FORCES OF
HORDES
MINIONS

CREDITS

HORDES created by
Matt Wilson

Project Director
Bryan Cutler

Game Design
Matt Wilson

Lead Designer
Jason Soles

Additional Development
David Carl
Brian Putnam

Art Direction
Kris Aubin

Lead Writer
Douglas Seacat

Additional Writing
Simon Berman
David Carl
Matt DiPietro
Ron Kruzie
Aeryn Rudel
Jason Soles
Matt Wilson

Continuity
Douglas Seacat
Jason Soles

Editing
Darla Kennerud
Sheelin Arnaud

Cover Illustration
Andrea Uderzo

Illustrations
Abrar Ajmal
Mike Bruinsma
Carlos Cabrera
Brian Despain
Matt Dixon
Emrah Elmasli
Mariusz Gandzel
David Kuo
Brian Snoddy
Andrea Uderzo
Kieran Yanner

Concept Illustration
Ben McSweeny
Chris Walton
Matt Wilson

Graphic Design & Layout
Kris Aubin
Shona Fahland
Kim Goddard
Josh Manderville
Stuart Spengler

Studio Director
Ron Kruzie

Miniature Sculpting
Steve Buddle
James Carter
Greg Clavilier
Benoit Cosse
Jason Hendricks
Werner Klocke
Aragorn Marks
Nicolas Nguyen
Edgar Ramos
Jose Roig
Steve Saunders
Ben Siens
Key White

Resin Caster
Sean Bullough

Miniature Painting
Matt DiPietro
Ron Kruzie
Allison McVey
Quentin Smith

Hobby Manager
Rob Hawkins

Terrain
Alfonzo Falco
Rob Hawkins

Photography
Kris Aubin
Rob Hawkins
Stuart Spengler

Development Manager
David Carl

President
Sherry Yeary

Chief Creative Officer
Matt Wilson

Creative Director
Ed Bourelle

Executive Assistant
Chare Kerzman

Project Manager
Shona Fahland

Marketing Coordinator
William Shick

Retail Support and Development
Ross Thompson

Customer Service
Adam Johnson

Events Coordinator
Jason Martin

Community Manager & Staff Writer
Simon Berman

Volunteer Coordinator
Jen Ikuta

No Quarter EIC
Aeryn Rudel

Licensing & Contract Manager
Brent Waldher

Production Director
Mark Christensen

Technical Director
Kelly Yeager

Production Manager
Doug Colton

Production
Max Barsana
Alex Chobot
Jack Coleman
Cody Ellis
Joel Falkenhagen
Joe Lee
Michael McIntosh
Reese Nash
Nick Scherdnik
Nate Scott
Jacob Stanley
Benjamin Tracy

Sys Admin/Webmaster
Chris Ross

Infernals
Jeremy Galeone
Peter Gaublomme
Joachim Molkow
Brian Putnam
Gilles Reynaud
Donald Sullivan

Playtest Coordinator
David Carl

Internal Playtesters
Simon Berman
Ed Bourelle
David Carl
Jack Coleman
Bryan Cutler
Dave Dauterive
Michael Faciane
Ben Misenar
Douglas Seacat
William Shick
Jason Soles
Brent Waldher
Chris Walton

External Playtesters
Alex Badion
Andrew Brandt
Brad Casey
David Dankel
Eric Ernewein
Logan Fisher
Steve Fortson
Jeremy Galeone
Peter Gaublomme
Tommy Geuns
Devon Goda
Andrew Hartland
Andrew Inzenga
Nick Kendall
Jeff Long
Wout Maerschalck
Rob Miles
Dirk Pintjens
Own Rehrauer
Jarred Robitaille
Josh Saulter
John Simon
Tim Simpson
Mark Thomas

Proofreading
Darla Kennerud
William Shick

ADAPT AND SURVIVE

FACTION BACKGROUND

Beyond the struggles of empires, dragons, and ancient cabals, other creatures of the wilds are caught up in the bloody struggles of western Immoren. Some seek profit from warfare and strife; others are tribal groups willing to offer their strength of arms in return for protection or supplies. Events can even sweep up the unaligned against their will as they are captured, enslaved, or coerced into doing the bidding of those more numerous or powerful.

Whatever their concerns or motivations, minions are an unknown element capable of catching enemies off-guard. From the primitive alchemy of swamp gobbers to Gudrun the Wanderer's drunken rages, from Alten Ashley's tremendous hunting rifle to Brun Cragback's armor-plated bear, the minions of the wilds are truly a diverse lot.

As conflicts intensify in their once-isolated lands, members of some of these wild races have begun to band together and fight under their own banners. The rugged farrow of the Thornfall Alliance charge into battle with rifles, cannons, axes, and clubs, ready to weather the brunt of any enemy assault. The vicious scaled gatormen have gathered as the Blindwater Congregation and bring swift death to those who venture into the swamps.

PLAYING MINIONS

Much like the dark religion of their mist-shrouded swamps, the Gatormen of the Blindwater Congregation are a curious blend of strength and subtlety. The amphibious Gator warriors and hulking warbeasts of the congregation bring undeniable strength to the battlefield, but their Bog Trog and Swamp Gobber allies, dark magic, and manipulation of the swamp itself lend a stealthy element that allows them to strike quickly and decisively before returning to the darkness beneath the swamp's placid surface.

In contrast, the Farrow of the Thornfall Alliance do not rely on ambushes or stealth but on blasting powder and a frenzy of clubs and cleavers. Lord Carver's forces bring a great number of firearms to the battlefield, useful in laying down a hail of bullets to stop enemies in their tracks while armored War Hogs anchor the lines. Farrow warlocks are adept at supporting these patchwork monsters that cleave any survivors into bite-size chunks. Whether by hiring freelance killers, lending your strength to the congregation of the shallows, or extending the reach of Lord Carver, it's time to . . .

Let Loose the Minions of War!

TABLE OF CONTENTS

Visit: www.privateerpress.com

Privateer Press, Inc. 13434 NE 16th St. Suite 120 • Bellevue, WA 98005
Tel (425) 643-5900 • Fax (425) 643-5902

For online customer service, email frontdesk@privateerpress.com

The river steamer *Alton Alre* churned its way through the night as it made its way south along the Black River. It required a confident pilot to navigate the currents in the darkness, although the moon Calder was almost full and the stars added their own luminescence to the languid surface. *Alton Alre* boasted some of the finest crewmen who had ever traversed the Black River, and they prided themselves on being able to travel day and night on any portion of the journey.

There were few luxury passenger riverboats running this stretch in recent years; intermittent warfare had made several sections of the river dangerous. In the north there was the chance of interference or even seizure by the Cygnaran or Khadoran Armies. Here in the south, the Protectorate's Menite zealots might take it upon themselves to make an example of any vessel heading toward Caspia. Most ships still made it through, and most attacks were on heavily laden supply vessels, but the wars had diminished demand for passenger traffic. The captain of the *Alton Alre* aimed to provide an experience no other ship could offer. He had gone so far as to install small swivel cannons fore and aft and hired a group of well-armed mercenaries to protect the ship. Thus far, luck had been with them and they had evaded serious trouble.

Along with a skilled pilot, safe running at night relied on keen-eyed spotters up front to watch for debris in the channel. The mate currently standing post was a serious boy fourteen years of age they called Solemn Sid. He had the eye for such work and had demonstrated proper patience, seeming to find no discomfort standing at the prow hour after hour scanning the water. This night while squinting ahead he saw several large logs lying across the waterway, likely fallen trees from the most recent storm. He blew on the whistle hanging around his neck to warn the pilot's house. After a short delay the great steam-powered wheels reversed to churn in the other direction, slowing the vessel's otherwise indomitable advance.

Sid seized hold of the longest boat hook on hand and scrambled over the rail, leaning forward to nudge the nearest log to see if they were floating loose or stuck. Something felt wrong about the way the hook struck the log's surface—it almost did not even feel like bark. Before he could consider this, what he had thought was a log erupted from the water and whirled toward him with a giant, open fang-filled mouth and cold, reptilian eyes. The first great bite of that mouth took off his arm above the elbow and shattered the wooden boat hook handle. Sid tumbled into the river and emitted only a water-choked gasp before he was pulled under. The river churned, but the night's darkness hid the red of blood upon the foam.

Scaled creatures emerged from the water around the ship and latched onto its hull with clawed hands before clambering up the sides. Bipedal reptilian figures wielding axe-bladed polearms rushed from the nearest shore and swept around to both sides. They swiftly made their way onto the vessel even as someone began frantically ringing an alarm bell. Gunfire erupted from several quarters as the boat's mercenary protectors scrambled to intercept. The cannons both fore and aft sounded, but then the crews manning them were quickly set upon.

The mercenaries took to the decks and fired their pistols into the faces of the oncoming gatormen but were forced to switch to blades as the scaled warriors closed. The crewmen seized whatever weapons they could find to confront the nightmare creatures, which seemed to shrug off their blows. Despite valiant efforts, the humans did not last long. Reptiles surged down the decks, killing everyone in their path. Screams filled the formerly peaceful night when the attackers reached the passengers. A number of people leapt into the waters to try to escape, only to find hungry and fang-filled jaws waiting below.

The great hall was made of roughhewn wood, but its interior had been carved and polished with greater attention. Its scope and grandeur went well beyond the standard of every other rickety hovel in the large farrow compound. The hall held a single enormous room, with a vaulted ceiling lost into darkness. Hooks along the walls displayed trophies gathered from dozens of past victories.

Long, broad slabs of wood were laid out across stone supports crossing the bulk of the main floor, each heaped with roasted carcasses or thick cuts of meat that oozed blood, having been only quickly charred on the fire pits. The air was dense with the smell of meat, smoke, and the farrow themselves. Dozens of warriors sat in uncomfortable silence as they stared toward the elevated stone throne at the back of the hall.

The Bringer of Most Massive Destruction occupied this seat: Lord Carver, Esquire III, who glared down at his subordinates with a menacing expression intended to be benevolent. Most of the gathered warriors avoided meeting his stare, fearing it would be seen as an impertinent challenge. Instead they eyed his left hand upon the hilt of his great chopping blade, called the Hand of God, which rested point downward adjacent to his seat of power. A limping, scrawny farrow dressed in tatters stepped forward with a clay platter and, trembling, raised it for Lord Carver's inspection. Atop it was a single cut of bleeding meat skewered by a two-pronged fork. Carver lifted the slice, casually tossed it into his mouth, and chewed noisily. He swallowed and nodded to the onlookers throughout the hall, raising his right hand graciously.

Immediately the room erupted with commotion as the gathered warriors lurched into motion, seizing the food in front of them with pleased snorts. The chiefs, seated at intervals to give each one distance from his rivals, claimed their meat first; their lieutenants followed suit next. Any of those who were too eager received jabs with serving forks or knives for their insolence. The sounds of farrow noisily chomping meat and sucking juices filled the hall as each warrior focused on filling his belly. Rough metal goblets were tended by the meek, injured, and maimed farrow forced to serve the tables. A variety of stolen ales, wine, and harder spirits were sloshed into these goblets at random and just as quickly guzzled by the gathered host. It was a tradition to celebrate every great victory with such a feast, and by farrow custom the rest could not eat until the highest chief had taken the first cut.

The large hall supported only a third of the chiefs, lieutenants, and battle shamans leading Lord Carver's fighting force. To accommodate all his leaders, he had already hosted this feast twice before. He had eaten his fill at the first gathering and therefore took only a symbolic bite in those that followed. Despite the tedium of enduring three nearly identical feasts, it was vital his subordinates shared this ritual and held their hunger in check until he let them feed. Some of his chiefs bristled at waiting—they were accustomed to eating the first cut, before the warriors of their individual tribes. Being forced to abase themselves now reminded them of their lesser standing within the Thornfall Alliance. Here a chief was only a leader of a group of warriors, and all chiefs bowed to Lord Carver.

Lord Carver watched them restlessly, feeling the itch for battle and conquest. He was already mentally assessing his next possible targets and contracts for hire. Recent successes had brought riches to his entire host, but Carver was not yet satisfied. His goals were more exalted and required constant effort to advance. Lord Carver was not content to be a petty lord or mercenary. He was determined to become a true king, and a king must have vast lands to call a kingdom.

The far doors of the hall banged open, allowing a sliver of bright sunlight to slice through the darker, smoky confines of the hall. Lord Carver growled and raise a hand to shield his eyes. Several battle-scarred farrow warriors barged into the hall. The few diners who glanced at the arrivals quickly decided the interruption was not significant enough to disturb their meal.

Lord Carver felt a lurking presence to his left and glanced in that direction to see that Dr. Arkadius had appeared from the shadowed region behind the throne. The human arcanist looked out of place in the hall, not only for his race but also for his strange attire. In addition to the fur-trimmed jacket he wore even in this hot climate, he bore a peculiar apparatus connecting an assortment of tubes and vials to the needled weapon he carried. Most farrow eyed him warily, steering clear. The human felt obliged to attend the feasts but was too squeamish to participate. Lord Carver knew humans to be dainty eaters that picked at their food like birds.

The warrior in the lead approached the throne. He offered a curt nod and then spoke loudly to be heard over the din, "Lord Carver!"

One of Carver's foremost subordinates, Chieftan Kortef, stepped forward and smashed the butt of his long spear into the back of the warrior's legs, making him topple forward onto the floor. "Show some respect, shoat! Who do you think you address?"

The warrior glared at Kortef but then prostrated himself. "Bringer of Most Massive Destruction, Lord Carver . . ." Seeing no immediate violent reprisals, he continued in a rush. "Gatormen! Past the river markers, my lord! A whole army!"

> ## "ARKADIUS, YOU FORGET YOUR PLACE. WHEN I NEED YOUR OPINION I WILL ASK FOR IT."

Lord Carver leaned forward with a severe scowl, and a number of the farrow nearest the throne stopped eating to listen, several still holding pieces of bleeding meat in their grease-covered hands. Territorial violations were no trivial matter in farrow culture, particularly among the chiefs. Carver demanded, "Where was this?"

Seeing he had his lord's interest, the warrior gave an account of the incursion. The report had come from a small section of the Black River in the northern Marchfells that the farrow had claimed just months earlier. When Lord Carver heard about the specific area concerned, his expression soured to a grimace.

He turned to beckon another figure lurking in the shadows on the opposite side of his throne from Dr. Arkadius. A female bone grinder named Johla obediently approached, her head bowed. Her leather garb was arrayed with dozens of carved bone totems. Tattoos in countless swirling fine lines traced along her face and arms to create patterns where her light fur would not grow; similar swirling patterns were inscribed into the enamel of the small tusks protruding from her lips. She was one of the few female farrow high in Lord Carver's inner circle, and Arkadius had selected her to oversee the mapping of the warlord's expanding domain. Carver demanded, "This place—I have claimed it? Some swamp?" His voice was skeptical and accusatory.

Johla showed no fear of her master, a contrast to most of the warriors and chiefs present. "Yes, that is your land. We had problems with the gatormen there. Seized that land and set markers. You decided to claim a piece of the river and the swamp so they knew you were serious. Take some of *their* lands, not just those useful to us." When he continued to glare, she added with a sigh, "It was your idea, not mine."

Lord Carver snorted. "I think I remember . . ."

Word spread among the farrow chiefs, and even more turned their attention to the conversation. Their interest was easier to capture now that they had worked their way through most of the feast. The most prestigious chiefs had sat back, hands on full stomachs, allowing their lieutenants to gorge themselves on the remainder of the food. Many eyes were upon Lord Carver now.

One of the most impertinent chiefs rose from his table and stamped a hoof. "Such an insult cannot pass unanswered!" Carver glared at him until he shrank back among his peers, who clapped him on the back for his courage in voicing what they were thinking.

Lord Carver tightened his grip on the hilt of his cleaver and brooded as the others waited, hardly breathing. He did not wish to waste time and warriors on some insignificant stretch of river. There were more important battles, and he had already been planning to march elsewhere. Dr. Arkadius interrupted his thoughts. "Ahem. Lord Carver . . ." As always, the human's voice sounded condescending to the warlord's ear, and he spoke loudly enough that his words carried to the room. "I advise against this fool's errand. There is nothing of interest in that region. Doubtless the gatormen are simply passing through, and the intrusion in your territory is accidental. Attacking would result in casualties for no gain."

Lord Carver's temper rose. The man's opinions carried weight with the farrow, but there were times it would be best if he kept them to himself. Dr. Arkadius was respected for delivering the enormous steam-powered war hogs into their army's arsenal. By his efforts battle-ready fighting boars had been bred and augmented, allowing for additional gun boars to be outfitted. Yet there was a widespread concern among the chiefs that the doctor had too much influence over decisions. Carver saw the reaction of his subordinates to

Arkadius' words as discussions amid the tables intensified. He saw disdain on the faces of many: their lips drew back in sneers, and they snorted disapprovingly.

Worse, Arkadius had spoken what Lord Carver had already been thinking. Lord Carver heard muttering from one of the nearby tables suggesting Arkadius was once again meddling in decisions that should be left to their lord. This pushed his temper past the boiling point. "Enough!" Lord Carver bellowed, his voice ringing loudly enough to shake dust loose from the wooden rafters. The muttering silenced, and the farrow warlord turned his rage-filled eyes on the doctor. "Arkadius, you forget your place. When I need your opinion I will ask for it."

Arkadius' face was calm, showing no evident fear. "Of course, it is your decision. The things I said are no less true. You are intelligent enough to recognize that."

Lord Carver stood abruptly from his throne and stepped closer to the human, looming over him with fists clenched. The man appeared unflinching, but he gripped his needled weapon as if ready to use it. Carver knew the thing could paralyze with a single injection. "You had better watch your tongue, Arkadius."

Too late, the man lowered his voice. "My advice was sincere; I meant no insult. I am here because you value my opinions and my work. Throwing away lives over a patch of swampland is obviously ridiculous."

Carver sneered and spoke at a similarly low level. "If it is so obvious, perhaps you should trust me to see it. I am no fool, Arkadius. Next time you have such thoughts, bring them to me more quietly."

"Well, at least we are in agreement on this." The human's tone was smug.

Lord Carver's eye darted back to the hall, where a third of his gathered chiefs and lieutenants watched tensely, awaiting his order. The last place he wanted to march them was the marsh river. But there was another factor to weigh, an element to which the scientist was blind: the hearts of his warriors, their loyalty and devotion to him. They must believe in his strength. Some of them already thought him influenced by Arkadius. This was more than galling; it was dangerous. The farrow must see there was no one above Lord Carver and his mind was his own. Further, he must prove he was a lord who would defend his territory against any invasion.

"No." He felt pleasure at the disbelief in Arkadius' eyes. He turned and let his voice boom across the smoky hall. "The intrusion will be met with force! The gatormen will pay in blood!" There was a great eruption as farrow scrambled to their hooves, the whole assembly stomping,

shouting, and striking their hands or goblets onto the tables rhythmically. Carver continued over the din, "Gather your warriors! Spread word to those not here. Be ready to march before I gather my beasts or your necks will feel the bite of my blade!"

They pushed open the great doors and swept from the chamber with rowdy enthusiasm, eager as ever for battle. The clamor of discordant horns rang out shortly thereafter. Lord Carver turned to Arkadius, whose expression was inscrutable. The scientist shook his head and said, "While you attend this foolishness I shall be occupied with more important matters in my laboratory."

"No!" Carver glowered at him. "You join us, to show your loyalty." The warlord jabbed a thick-nailed finger into the other warlock's chest. "But stay in back. See to the war hogs and gun boars. I will teach you about farrow. You know our flesh, but not our minds. I will show you."

Carver jumped down from the dais, the floor shuddering beneath his weight, and strode out of the hall. Flies had already begun to buzz above the scattered bones left strewn across the tables. After a short pause he heard footsteps behind him as the human scrambled to catch up.

After the great slaughter the gatormen and their beasts retired to the nearby shore to digest. An overlapping low droning filled the air, mixed with a hissing that rose and fell in cycles. It was the sound of dozens of bokors raising their voices in chant-like ritual. They were scattered along the blood-soaked shore of the river, staring up at the baleful moons and the distant, wan stars. The river was once again placid, but grisly evidence of the riverboat massacre drifted periodically to rest amid the reeds and cattails nearer the shore or floated silently downstream deeper into the Marchfells.

The bokors' ominous chant was hypnotically regular, but its timbres could not be produced by human voices; it was the sound of some ancient and unwholesome gatorman ritual. The air itself was leaden with unnatural malignancy, as if the fetid atmosphere of the swamp were manifesting as a tangible thing. Those gatormen possessing particular sensitivity to the spirit world could see flickers of nebulous forms rising from the river to gather in clusters near those who chanted, drawn to their bone-festooned weapons and talismans.

The masked gatorman bokor called Calaban, the Grave Walker, observed the proceedings from farther back, at the center of a ring of smoking torches. Calaban held a polished crystal skull through which he peered at the

and he stammered, "Great One, have mercy! I live to serve!" This time he placed proper emphasis on the honorific, and his posture suggested humility.

"Send your tadpoles in both directions along the riverbank." Calaban pointed to illustrate. "It will be your task to warn us—of soldiers approaching or any armed threat. Also watch for large boats. Any you see, send a runner to me." He released the trog and let him gather his tribe. With burbling mutters they dispersed in either direction: some to the south, others north along the shore. In the low light their skin blended into the reeds, and they quickly vanished from sight.

Calaban saw a gatorman lurking at the perimeter of his ring of torches, a familiar older warrior from one of the local tribes that had just recently joined them. He carried a long, ugly scar along the left side of his face as well as evidence of other battle wounds, but he had proven to be somewhat reluctant to devote himself to the cause. Furthermore, he was in the habit of pestering Calaban with inconsequential suggestions. The warlock addressed him now without turning his gaze from the crystal skull. "What is it, seth-hetlin Lagshin?" A seth-hethlin was a leader of a hunting expedition, a mild honorific Calaban allowed him with obvious reluctance.

The old warrior kept his head averted respectfully and spoke with some hesitation. "I should warn you, great bokor Calaban, we have come too far north. We passed certain territorial markers, farrow markers. I tried to tell your bokors. By now, the farrow scouts will have seen us."

Calaban growled. He had no interest in the petty territorial arrangements of the locals. "Why should I care about these markers? Whatever boundaries your village once agreed to heed, they do not apply to our congregation." Behind Calaban, wallowing in the muddy waters, a hulking blackhide wrastler swung its head around to peer at the old warrior, its eyes gleaming. It slithered behind Calaban and opened its jaws in a threatening posture toward the warrior supplicant, who stepped back in fear.

dance of spirits that arose to the beckoning chants of the lesser bokors. This ritual had been arranged to his specifications, and he watched it with a critical eye. When he was interrupted by creatures bringing him information or requesting further orders, he dealt with each with the cool efficiency of one whose mind could effectively focus on many tasks at once.

He emitted an imperious clacking noise from deep in his throat and gestured sharply at a cluster of bog trogs. They were huddled clannishly at the back of the clearing gulping down what scraps had been allowed them by the gatormen. Their leader, attired in ornate armor assembled from turtle shells, approached Calaban warily. His posture suggested submission, but his bright eyes carried the spark of a more defiant spirit. This bog trog had once been a mighty chief of his people, before Calaban had forced his surrender. It had required the murder of his mate and his offspring to take the fight from him.

"Yes, great one . . ." The words of their shared language were pronounced quite differently by the trogs, and this one's enunciation of the honorific suggested insult. The insolent bog trog likely expected a gatorman not to notice, but Calaban had a keen ear. The warlock extended his weapon to hook its razor-sharpened-bone edges behind the creature's neck. The trog's mouth widened in surprise

Lagshin swept his tail away and lowered his torso in submission. "The chief who leads these farrow is unusually strong. He has many followers, and they are vengeful, great bokor. I mention this only to forewarn you. They will think my village has broken our agreements and will come to punish us."

"Do you believe I or Barnabas cannot endure an attack by farrow?" Calaban had not been looking at the old warrior but now turned sharply to face him, his expression mirroring that of the wrastler. "Do you believe we are too weak?"

"No, no, not too weak! No. I only warn, so you know they may come. Forgive me, Grave Walker. I serve the Congregation."

"Prove your devotion in the next battle. Bring your village bokor and your posse. There will be more ships soon. Warriors of your village will enter the fray first."

Lagshin debased himself further and slithered away, reduced to crawling in the mud like an ordinary alligator in his efforts not to give offense. Calaban hissed in irritation. The local gatormen would fall fully under Barnabas' sway eventually, but becoming true believers did not happen overnight. Until then he must suffer their irksome questions and ensure they kept to their place.

Even as the old warrior departed and Calaban raised the crystal skull to his eye once more there was a sudden familiar weight upon the back of his mind, a spiritual power so great it imposed itself upon the world around it. The flames of his smoking torches guttered and several extinguished outright, and the clear gleaming crystal he held became darkened and opaque.

Calaban turned to see Bloody Barnabas, who had silently entered the circle behind him. Calaban's attending gatorman warriors standing guard just outside the torches had dropped to their most submissive postures for this, the absolute master of the Blindwater Congregation. As always, the ancient bokor walked with a certain disregard for his surroundings, as if it were mere accident he had come to this place. Upon his back were several rods to which were affixed human skulls; to Calaban's mystical vision these were filled with dense knots of black power that seemed to leech warmth and light from the world. They were fulcrums channeling the spiritual energies of death and annihilation.

The Grave Walker's stance changed almost instantly. In his previous meetings he had stood erect and commanding, but now he folded inward, lowering his torso and turning his fearsome mask and fanged maw away and down. It was a show of humility only Barnabas could provoke in him.

The ancient bokor seemed not to notice but spoke in resonant and hissing tones. "Calaban. I grow restless. Shall we return to Blindwater? These southern swamps are tedious."

Calaban wrung his hands in agitation but then forced himself to control the gesture. Answering, he offered the honorific ordinarily reserved for the greatest of the manifested spirits with which the bokors sometimes negotiated. "Great hok-shisan, oblige me a little longer. Allow another great ship, perhaps two, to fall beneath your bite before we depart this place. This river is swollen with spirits drawn to bloodshed."

Barnabas turned to face him with particular swiftness, his axe in hand, his posture suggesting great agitation. "You asked to conduct a ritual requiring the slaughter of many humans. This we have done."

"A bit more is all we require, hok-shisan. It will be worth some patience, I assure you."

Barnabas made a rumbling noise deep in his throat. "You pressed me to come to these southern lands to recruit among your villages. I start to suspect other motives. Are you not the voice of caution? With this slaughter, will we not attract human armies? It seems reckless for you, Calaban." Barnabas' voice remained laconic, suggesting he had no concern for the risks he named. Calaban understood it was only his motives that were under scrutiny.

"The humans will be slow to learn of the fate of this ship. We left no survivors. At least two days before we need be concerned about patrols investigating, and we will be gone by then. By your leave I ask—I entreat!—that my work continue a little longer. Our bokors will take significant strength from the harvest."

Barnabas tilted his head as if listening to something only he could hear. "Nothing is important or relevant except my ascension. I do not see how this slaughter serves *me*."

Calaban protested smoothly, "I assure you, hok-shisan, your ascension is foremost on my mind! These steps will solidify your name and reputation. We flaunt our strength close to one of the human fortresses, turning the river to blood. The stronger our bokors, the more aid they can lend in your battles to come. We cannot stop with one paltry vessel."

Barnabas eyed him skeptically and raised a scaled hand toward the chanting bokors. "This ritual seems well prepared, Calaban. It is ornate and unfamiliar. You presented this as an opportunity of convenience. Now, I wonder. How long have you been planning this?"

Calaban listened with growing apprehension; Barnabas could halt the endeavor at any time. The recent passage of a dragon flying over this region had stirred the spirits here in a way that might never happen again. Calaban had invested tremendous time and effort in unearthing the lore that had brought him to this place—too much to allow Barnabas' mercurial moods to spoil his plans. If he decided to withdraw, the gatormen would follow and Calaban would be forced to abandon his work. He did not answer the question directly. "A little more patience, hok-shisan."

Barnabas stood still a long time, as Calaban's apprehension of danger heightened. At times like this, Barnabas sometimes delivered swift death, rarely giving any hint of his temper before he struck. Calaban thought himself beyond such considerations, but he knew the folly of trying to predict the mind of one as ancient and deranged as Barnabas.

Eventually the venerable bokor turned away. "I will indulge you again, Calaban. But know I am not blind to your schemes." With that the gatorman bokor who aspired to become a god strode away. As he passed, the remaining torches set by Calaban extinguished in sputters of thick smoke.

The farrow had reached the river and determined the gatormen had moved farther north, escalating their intrusion. Lord Carver and his army followed the banks in that direction, enduring the uncertain, marshy ground and the dense vegetation. Soon they spotted debris floating down the river. Arkadius and the bone grinders came forward to inspect a particularly large section of flotsam and scattered corpses that had washed up along the shore in a small inlet.

"This seems to be the wreckage of more than one riverboat." Dr. Arkadius mused. He pointed at the aft section of some vessel that had been entirely shattered. "There, I see painted text. The *Graceful Swan*. I booked passage on that vessel once. The captain was exceedingly rude—"

"Why are gatormen attacking human boats?" Lord Carver interrupted the arcanist. "What is the meaning of this battle?"

"Not a battle—a massacre." The farrow nearby shifted uneasily and muttered superstitiously until Lord Carver silenced them with a glare. The human continued, "The bodies are dismembered but not chewed to the bone, so clearly it was not food they needed. But who can fathom the minds of reptiles? Why does the snake bite the heel of a man just passing by? There is no benefit from attacking ships here, unless they hoped to provoke a reaction from Fort Falk to the north."

"I'm not looking to do Cygnar any favors," Lord Carver groused. His ears flicked in irritation.

"You were the one who felt obliged to defend this obscure corner of your territory. If we were going to defend Cygnaran river trade, I would suggest we get paid for our troubles."

Lord Carver made a grumbling noise in his throat.

Both of them looked up sharply at shouts made by farrow farther up the river. A sudden eruption of rifle fire echoed from ahead. Several of the razorback crews looked back for direction, clearly wondering if they should prepare their weapons. Lord Carver waved them forward. "Not until you see something worth shooting! Keep moving!" The farrow warlord ran past them, his huge blade in hand, as other farrow parted hastily to make way for him and the three massive war hogs rushing to keep up behind him.

Lord Carver reached the trees. The bodies strewn ahead told him how the fight had transpired. Several gatorman corpses riddled with holes were bleeding out in the reeds nearby, each surrounded by a number of hacked-apart farrow brigands. It looked as though the gatormen had struck upon them from the cover of the trees and delivered brutally efficient attacks before withdrawing. Dozens of freshly arrived farrow had hunkered down amid the vegetation near the corpses and were taking turns firing blindly into the trees.

"What are you shooting at? Shadows?" Lord Carver felt a surge of blood lust imagining the retreating gatormen. "Get after them, cowards! Into the trees!" The nearest warriors looked chagrined at his words and hastened to obey, leaving their covered positions. Carver saw Arkadius had caught up with him, bringing his own war hog and gun boars. "We have them on the run!"

Dr. Arkadius frowned in skepticism. "Reptiles do not feel fear as we do. I would be cautious in your presumptions."

Lord Carver barked a laugh and shouted back, "*Now* you know how they think?" He hurried ahead, eager to let his blade drink the blood of the foe.

Plunging between the low-hanging trees, he pushed through the reeds to splash into a deeper mire of brackish water thick with rank weeds and rotting vegetation. The muddy soil sucked at his hooves, and strands of vine wrapped his legs. He growled in annoyance, seeing his farrow similarly hindered. Ahead he saw the gatormen, not retreating as he had expected but backing away from them, weapons in hand. They were hissing at one another and appeared calm, their efforts coordinated. Lord Carver considered Arkadius' words but pushed the warning aside. True, the gatormen did not look afraid—but what did his army have to fear from a local village of such creatures, however individually hardy?

Brigands fired at the reptiles, some shots hitting but most missing their targets in the murky darkness amid the vegetation. Lord Carver drew on the repressed rage built up in his war hogs. He raised his weapon, the Hand of God, and unleashed primal energy that empowered the muscles of his legs as well as those of his war hogs. By this sorcery they stepped through the swamp as if striding across an open plain, the undergrowth and water no longer obstructing them. With a great cry, he charged forward alongside his beasts. His brigands stayed behind and provided cover fire. They would all witness as he dealt with the enemy personally.

His sudden speed was unexpected by the gatormen, who attempted too late to begin their own counter charge. He met them on his terms, bringing down the Hand of God to carve through both thick, scaly hide and bone with equal ease. He felt his blood stir and his heart race as gatormen came to meet him with snapping jaws, swinging their own weapons. He dodged beneath a wild swipe and neatly decapitated that gatorman with a sideways hack of his blade that sent the head spinning bloodily through the air to splash into the murky water.

One of the gatormen on his left managed to seize his arm in its toothy maw and bit deeply. Lord Carver gave a howl of rage but yanked loose, feeling the fangs rip ragged tears along his flesh. He accepted the injury rather than shunt it to his war hog, which charged the one that had injured him and ended its life with a single downward chop of one of its massive axes. His other war hogs barreled into the gatormen closing on him. Steam engines howled as machine-powered arms that had once been affixed to warjacks made swift work of the gators, adding to the acrid smell of freshly spilled blood. A great shout went up from his brigands.

A gatorman festooned with feathers and wearing a vest assembled of human rib-bones gave a grating call, gesturing frantically. The gatormen pulled back again. Those Carver did not immediately hack down with his weighty blade turned to flee. He reached over his shoulder to draw his sawed-off scattergun; firing both barrels he sent metal scrap through two of the fleeing gatormen to his left. One fell but the other limped on through the reeds, which closed behind it. The mist rising from the murky swamp enveloped them while the peculiar throaty calls of unknown birds were heard in the near distance.

Only Bloody Barnabas dared approach Calaban while the Grave Walker was so deep in trance, his mind at one with the malevolent spirits enslaved to his will. "A farrow army approaches. Your bog trogs say they are well armed." Barnabas' voice did not sound concerned, simply irritated at having to consider such trivial information. "Time to leave this place."

Calaban's expression and attention did not waver, but he felt a moment of panic as the great spell he was constructing began to falter. It was a crucial moment in the ritual. Considerable force of will was required just to stay within his own mind long enough to speak, let alone convey the properly respectful tone and posture. "We are almost ready. . . So close. . . Lure the farrow here. . . All we require is a few more deaths."

Even speaking these words almost caused him to lose control of the ritual, which he could not risk. Ordinarily Calaban had no difficulty dividing his attention, but he had never attempted a work of this scale. He felt the pressure of Barnabas' lengthy consideration, as if the leader of the Blindwater Congregation were debating murdering him where he stood. Calaban knew there was little he would be able to do to defend himself, preoccupied as he was.

After what seemed an interminable time, the elder bokor turned away. "Very well. I will order them herded here. Pray this proves enlightening or amusing, Calaban. Your god cannot protect you from *me*."

Barnabas left without waiting for a reply. The masked shaman felt momentary relief even as he redoubled his efforts to control the wildly unpredictable energies he marshaled.

The farrow warlord gave chase, using his sorcery to speed his own steps as well as those of his warbeasts, refusing to let the enemy have any pause to rally and regroup. He left his warriors behind, although the shamans leading many of them belatedly began to chant prayers intended to speed their steps through the murk. The crewmen lugging the heavy razorbacks had no such benefit, and encumbered by their heavy weapons they lagged even farther behind. Yet Carver had set forth on this expedition to prove his willingness to take to battle and defend his territory personally, and with his war hogs at his side he felt unstoppable. Gatormen were fierce opponents, but they clearly had not anticipated what sort of enemy they had provoked. He had no patience to wait for his army to catch up to him.

Slightly dampening Lord Carver's enthusiasm was a wariness toward the rising fog and an unwillingness to engage in battle without his warriors present to witness his triumph. He heard farrow warriors and shamans behind him and whistled loudly to announce his position to them. From their scattered snorts and calls it seemed they had spread into the marsh, some led astray to the north. Eventually several small groups reached him and shook pig irons in salute. Together with his war hogs they marched through the misted reeds, which parted on a macabre display.

on the air. Despite the rising sun shining over the placid river, the light seemed feeble through the haze of fog and smoke.

Stepping forward from the riverbank was another gatorman who immediately conveyed the impression of being mightier than the rest. This bokor wielded a strange staff tipped with a gatorman skull and spiked with sharpened bones. Upon his face was a carved wooden mask, and he wore a loincloth of human skulls. In his hand, dangling from a cord set with quartz, was a large, carved crystal skull with orange gems for eyes. The bokor raised the crystal totem and hissed something in their base reptilian language, prompting glowing runes of power to encircle his hands. Immediately several of the gators on either side advanced, while other creatures began to rise up from the waters, including a pair of large, bipedal turtles with baleful eyes. The gatorman warriors charged forward with their bladed polearms raised.

Whatever mystical significance was attached to the chanting gatormen and this leading bokor, Lord Carver cared not.

Ahead was a large clearing, the entire area covered in several feet of murky water. Just past this stagnant pond and a narrow raised embankment was an inlet of the river itself. He could see its waters just behind a gathered throng of gatormen—more than he had anticipated, including over a dozen attired in ceremonial finery, their fanged maws raised in a strange chant. Torches lining the clearing and the river embankment burned with red, guttering flames that churned thick smoke into the air.

Huge piles of fresh bones littered the area, most still gory with tendons and scraps of muscle and flesh. Heads and skulls in various stages of decay were piled up by the dozens at the base of every torch, and rope rigging from plundered riverboats was stretched between the trees and strung with dangling femurs and arm bones. Massive alligators still worked on more recent bodies, tearing loose flesh to swallow. The smell of death and decay was heavy

He shouted for his warriors to fire. They raised their pig irons to trigger great blasts from the wide-bored weapons. Additional farrow arrived at the clearing, saw their leader, and quickly formed up into ranks. Their withering fire tore through a number of the gatormen and beasts and silenced several of the outer bokors. Yet the surviving gatorman warriors and smaller alligators closed on Lord Carver with surprising alacrity. The farrow warlord invoked his sorcery again, bolstering himself and his beasts with layers of protective magic that settled into their hides to toughen them and shield them from harm.

Even as the alligators and gatormen rushed in, the turtles emitted strange retching noises. Their heads jerked in a sudden motion as each spat a messy glob of fluid. One struck Carver's nearest war hog and the fluid sprayed across it, burning everything it touched. The war hog gave an angry bellow as the corrosive fluid began to eat through its skin despite Lord Carver's protective warding. The other gob of fluid splattered amid several of the farrow behind and to his right, making them shriek in pain and tear at their armor before falling to die thrashing in the water.

Carver sent one of his war hogs to charge the turtles and stop their acidic expectorations just as he and his remaining hogs were beset by alligators. The smaller bull snappers were not exceptionally hardy, but their bites tore through flesh with ease. Other snappers surged past them to spring upon the nearest farrow. Lord Carver brought his cleaver down to hack through one, but two more lunged at him, hissing.

More farrow entered the clearing from behind and laid down fire, but then these newcomers were beset by bog trogs flanking them from the wall of reeds and landing brutal blows with their metal-hooked poles. The entire clearing turned into a chaotic tumult of farrow, gators, and bog trogs. Many of Carver's bandits had to abandon pig irons and draw clubs to defend themselves in melee.

One of Lord Carver's war hogs faltered as bull snappers tore its legs out, and then a blackhide wrastler managed to rip its mechanikal arm off with a sickening sound of tearing flesh before hurling it into the water. Carver's mind was immersed in the indignant rage of his beasts as he sent the command for the aggression dials set into their chests to be turned to the highest settings. Vials of unnatural fluids emptied to flood their veins while their steam engines cranked to higher pressure. The hogs gave roars of anger and their eyes turned red as Arkadius' serums went into effect: their hearts beat overtime and their muscles strained, some even tearing loose from the bone. The empowered war hogs hacked their way through scaled flesh in a savage frenzy of axes, but there seemed no end to the enemy.

Lord Carver witnessed Dr. Arkadius arrive at last into the clearing with his own war hog and gun boars. The boars were directed to fire their crude cannons into the fray. Whatever his failings, the scientist was a good judge of distances and threats, and although his blasts sometimes exploded uncomfortably close to his allies, the shrapnel tore through only their enemies.

The farrow warlord fumed to see Arkadius staying back until he remembered his standing orders to the human. Swallowing his pride, he yelled, "Get down here!" Under bog trog attack from all directions, the farrow line was in tatters. There were as many trog as farrow corpses littering the rear of the clearing, but the situation looked to be growing steadily grimmer. Even as the warlord chopped into the enemies around him, additional bog trogs came streaming out of the river, making warbling cries.

Carver saw Arkadius demonstrate unexpected bravery by striding directly up to a massive blackhide wrastler to pierce it with his needle gun to paralyze it before letting his war hog hack it to pieces. The doctor invoked magic to tear through other enemies even as Carver was forced to be frugal with his own, focusing on defensive efforts and occasionally diverting his injuries to his beasts instead. Blood flowed down his sides, and multiple lacerations covered his arms, legs, and chest.

Several of the razorback crews had gotten into position and set their launching tubes firmly before sending the rockets to explode amid clusters of the bog trogs nearest the river. With the help of concentrated pig iron and gun boar fire, Dr. Arkadius and his war hog managed at last to open the ring around Lord Carver and give the embattled warlord a short respite. Even as his second war hog collapsed to die in the muck, he sensed they had made it through the worst of it. More reinforcing farrow rushed into the clearing.

The air was thick with smoke, and still the chanting rose—if anything, even stronger than before. Carver felt dizzy and disoriented amid the uproar, and he was having difficulty breathing. He was aware he had been unable to press the battle forward to confront the leading enemy warlock, who was still at the other side of the clearing working his extended mystical ritual. He could feel the magic tickling along his skin, building like a storm. The farrow warlord prepared to order his men to rush the bokors.

Lord Carver's ears were ringing from the sounds of exploding razorback rockets and the many crackling reports of pig irons when suddenly an eerie silence overtook the swamp, broken only by the bokor's chanting. Looking around, Carver spotted the nearest gatormen and their beasts slipping quietly below the surface of the water to vanish. Then the chanting stopped. Carver stood ambivalent in the bloody mud- and gore-filled water, looking across the layer of corpses surrounding them, and wondered if they had actually provoked the remaining gators to flee. He mistrusted their peculiar retreat. His skin itched as his instincts told him his warriors were still in peril.

"Load weapons! Stand ready!" he shouted. More warriors of his army had found their way to his side, but it was still only a small assortment of his chiefs. His scattered squads were likely having trouble converging on his location.

Arkadius had moved nearer, and he looked alarmed as well. "Something is not right. . . Do you feel it?" He took a deep breath and then coughed.

Lord Carver realized the air was heavy not simply from the reek of death and blasting powder smoke but from something far stronger and fouler. Taking breaths became difficult, as if water entered his lungs with every draw. He coughed into his hand and saw blood. Lord Carver heard a strange sound. Through the parting mists he saw the masked warlock. The bokor stood with scaled arms raised, his bone scythe in one hand, the crystal skull in the other. A sickly, yellow glow now filled the crystal's interior, pulsing like a heartbeat. The warlock's head was turned upward, and a low noise from deep in his throat was the only sound. At last he lowered his masked face and looked directly at Carver, his eyes gleaming. Was the gatorman gloating?

Another imposing gatorman arrived, stepping past the heaped piles of freshly severed human heads. This one wielded an axe and had a leather cowl covering his head. On his back he wore an arrangement of spiked sticks atop which additional skulls rested. Power seemed to radiate palpably from him. Yet it was not the arriving bokor that froze the blood in Carver's veins and made him feel a tremor of uncertainty for the first time.

> ## LORD CARVER GAVE A BELLOW AND DROVE THE ENEMY WARLOCK BACK WITH A SEQUENCE OF FIERCE BLOWS.

Something enormously dark, spectral, and terrible rose wailing from the river depths to sweep into the clearing, blotting out the sun. The bones of dozens of corpses littering the clearing were pulled up to join the ghostly apparition. The masked gatorman warlock kept his hands upraised and bellowed an answering chant, while the other bokors blended their voices with his from the periphery. The spectral entity spread across the air above them as if trying to envelop the entire swamp, howling and pulsing in rhythm to the bokors' chants.

Lord Carver could gain only a vague impression of its shape and size, as it appeared translucent and amorphous to his eyes. It seemed insubstantial and yet black as night. It conveyed a sinuous, serpentine impression, and despite its formlessness he sensed something akin to a mouth lined with countless razor-sharp triangular teeth. The swamp itself seemed to respond to the entity's presence: the temperature in the clearing dropped severely, and the ground beneath the farrow became even more viscous and grasping, seizing their hooves and pulling them downward as if seeking to swallow them whole.

The air had grown thicker, and the spirit roared above them like a tornado. Suddenly the reptiles that had submerged beneath the water erupted from its surface with croaks and howls, their eyes maddened. Bog trogs and gatormen alike leapt forward as if in answer to the spirit's call, emitting unreal, angry roars. More bull snappers poured forth from the depths and charged with fervor. Their wild, frenzied movements seemed unnatural even in the thick of battle, and their reptilian eyes held only the glow of spirit-induced rage.

Behind him Carver heard squeals of alarm from the farrow brigands. They were stuck in the mud and water, with the swamp vines wrapped around their legs holding fast like rope. They attempted to fire their pig irons at the enemy closing on their warlord, but their rifles failed. Likewise, the rockets of the razorback crews were unresponsive to ignition efforts. The great, howling spirit had strangled and choked their weapons, perhaps drowning their powder with the unnaturally wet air.

The leather-cowled warlock wielding the hook-bladed axe stepped deliberately toward Lord Carver, followed by several gator warbeasts including a hulking blackhide wrastler. Carver realized that like the other farrow his legs were held fast in the grip of the swamp, and he was still laboring to breathe. Whatever malevolent force had been summoned seemed to paralyze him. The gatorman bokor coming toward him opened a mouth to show sharp teeth in what seemed a smile, as if savoring his discomfort, and then raised an axe to strike.

Carver drew on the anger within his war hog and then focused his will to free his feet from the mire and forced the war hog to tear itself clear. He narrowly evaded the first swing from the gatorman warlock and then brought his blade up to block the next slash. He retaliated with his own sweeping blows but found his enemy to be a skilled warrior able to evade and block his strikes with almost-casual ease. Meanwhile the blackhide wrastler leapt at his war hog, and the two began a deadly clash.

Seeing Lord Carver extract himself from the mire, Arkadius added the energy he derived from his beasts to his own force of will to free himself but was quickly beset. The scientist unleashed his power to slow one of the bull snappers closing on him with sorcerous chains, but a second snapper latched onto his leg. The human was forced to send his injuries onto his beasts in a desperate act as his enemies closed, including several gatorman warriors. Weakened by their own injuries as well as those shunted to them by Arkadius, his warbeasts began to falter and collapse despite his arcane efforts to seal their wounds. Preoccupied with the axe-wielding warlock, Carver barely saw Arkadius stumble and fall into the bloody water.

Feeling a sense of urgency, Carver willed his war hog to unleash a frenzy of chopping blows into the wrastler it was fighting. In its fury, the hog hacked the beast to pieces, but it suffered several deep wounds in return.

Lord Carver swung a powerful horizontal blow that would have severed his enemy's left arm if he had not pulled back in time to reduce it to a bleeding gash. They exchanged several blows, evading one another and retaliating in turn. Battling the warlock was made more difficult by the fact that in addition to the gator's axe, he had to worry about gnashing teeth and a powerfully muscled tail that could shatter bones on impact. Carver opened himself up to a crushing tail-strike to his leg in order to land a heavy downward chop into the enemy's shoulder, but the warlock simply diverted the wound to one of the many reptilian beasts in the waters. The leather-cowled gatorman seemed to be enjoying the clash, flashing his teeth in a sinister grin.

Carver knew he was in impossible circumstances. He had to get clear of the howling spirit above that had incapacitated his entire local force, and he believed that if he invoked his mobility magic he might have a chance. He could give himself a burst of speed and have the war hog distract the enemy long enough to ensure his escape.

Arkadius managed to regain his feet with the help of a maimed gun boar and staggered back from the fray alongside it. The human yelled to Lord Carver, "We need to retreat while we can! This battle is over!"

Something about hearing his previous thoughts voiced by Arkadius unnerved Lord Carver. He looked back to the farrow warriors stuck in the mud and being hacked down by gatormen. Some were valiantly fighting on, reduced to battering the enemy with their clubs. They had not broken or fallen into panic, since they could see him. They knew he yet stood. Lord Carver gave a bellow and drove the enemy warlock back with a sequence of fierce blows and then yelled back to the scientist, "No! The battle is not over until I say so! Find a way to deal with *that*!" He pointed a blood-dripping hand at the howling spirit above them but had to immediately return his attention to his enemy.

The gatorman warlock hissed loudly and swung a vicious blow that skittered off the top edge of Carver's cleaver and bit deeply into his side. Lord Carver ignored the pain and pressed on, smashing the enemy in the face with the pommel of Hand of God hard enough to shatter several teeth and send the gator staggering back, spraying bloody spittle. He urged his war hog forward to attack the warlock, buying himself a short reprieve to step back, appraise the situation, and apply his power to close some of his worst wounds.

Seeing Arkadius beset by yet more warbeasts, Carver stepped up and hacked into one before it could latch onto the injured human, who was limping on a badly lacerated leg. Arkadius was panting, but his expression suggested smugness. He grinned at Lord Carver and said, "Look how peculiar these reptiles are acting!" He waved to indicate those just outside their immediate circle of muddy and blood-infused water. "They turn on one another, driven to madness. The spirit

above is not fully under their control but pulls at their minds even as it grasps our warriors in its clutches."

Carver looked beyond them and saw that a strange light had come to the eyes of the gatormen and they were attacking wildly. Several fought one another, mindless of being allies. Behind them he saw bog trogs besetting gatormen as they, too, fell under the malevolent influence of the spectral abomination that had sprung from the river. At the center of the hurricane of swirling blackness stood the masked warlock with his hands upraised.

Lord Carver had not had time to wonder why this other warlock had not joined the clash. Now he perceived the leading bokor seemed to be engaged in a desperate mental struggle with the wailing entity above, and clearly it was not fully obedient to his will. The sudden flash of insight Lord Carver felt was followed by the awareness of his last war hog falling to the leather-cowled warlock he had sent it against. He looked up to see the gatorman wrenching his enormous axe free from the thick skull of the collapsed hog. The warlock glowered and stepped toward the pair, his expression dark and sinister. Lord Carver yelled to Arkadius, "Deal with him! I'll take the other!"

"What?" Arkadius seemed bewildered but could do nothing before the gatorman warlock was upon him. Lord Carver was already circling toward the masked bokor instead.

Arkadius yelped and leapt to the side as an axe came whistling down just inches from his face. Pulling on what remained of his flagging sorcerous energies, he invoked a binding magic on the gatorman to seize his muscles. He then jabbed his needle into the bokor's torso and injected powerful venoms into his reptilian bloodstream. This severely weakened the enemy warlock, who nevertheless still managed to strike home a brutal backhanded slash in retaliation. Sensing death closing in on him, the reeling human desperately sent part of this wound to his last gun boar, which toppled with its chest split open. The gatorman turned away from Arkadius as the human crumpled, apparently dismissing him as a threat.

The distraction had given the farrow warlord enough time to cross the intervening distance. One of the masked warlock's attending bodyguards stepped to intercept, but Carver hacked it in twain before it could even raise its weapon. Lord Carver drew his scattergun and fired both barrels straight into the chanting bokor's face. The wooden mask exploded into splinters, and both wood and shrapnel tore into the enemy's eyes and flesh. The warlock roared in pain and staggered back as he sent the injury to slay one of his nearby gator beasts. His chant was disrupted and his concentration was lost. The fanged spirit's defiant and triumphant scream filled the air.

The wind erupted at even greater strength, and rain sliced through the clearing like wet blades. The madness that had been afflicting the gatormen amplified, and they attacked one another with fiendish enthusiasm. With his blood dripping down into the swamp, Calaban felt the spirit create a wall of wind and rain that drove the farrow warlock away, into the path of one of the surviving ironback spitters.

Barnabas stepped up to loom over him, hissing in rage. "What have you done, Calaban? The battle turns against us!" The spirit's defense of Calaban had forced it to release its hold over the rest of the farrow, who were beginning to rally; their weapons were working for them once more, and they were hastily firing into the tumult of the maddened gatormen and bog trogs.

"It does not matter!" Calaban gasped. "I have it! It was my blood, the key . . ." His blood had dripped down his arm to coat the crystal skull, and by this personal sacrifice Calaban had felt the pact with the ancient reptilian spirit solidify. It had required an enormous price to awaken the long-forgotten thing, but now the spirit was his. He could feel it binding to his blood, his heart. By sheer strength of will he forced it to give up its manifested form and sink into the crystal skull.

"Come, you fool!" Barnabas growled as he yanked the other warlock toward the river. Exhausted from his effort, Calaban allowed himself to be dragged.

"Never fear, Barnabas—the losses we have suffered today do not matter compared to what we have gained."

Barnabas grumbled, "I hope so, Grave Walker, or I will make a trophy of your skull." The two of them and the rest of their surviving force entered the water's depths.

Lord Carver was knocked backward as the ironhide spitter smashed into his chest. Gritting his teeth against the pain of broken ribs, he staggered back to his feet and smashed Hand of God into the turtle's side, cracking through the armored shell. He yanked the blade free and hammered thrice more, until the creature lay in an obliterated heap at his feet.

Explosions filled the air as the razorbacks resumed their fire, sending rockets forward into the reptilian horde. This was soon joined by pig iron fire. The chanting of farrow shamans urged the warriors on, and they swept the field of the gatormen. Lord Carver strode alongside them,

searching for either of the bokor warlocks who had led this effort. Briefly, he glimpsed what could have been the one holding the crystal skull sinking into the water of the Black River to fade from sight, but he put that aside. The marsh was filled with the flesh of alligator and farrow corpses, and he'd had enough of chasing after reptiles in the muck. The enemy was driven off, decisively.

The farrow let loose a jubilant howl as they realized the enemy was defeated, and then Lord Carver was seized in rough hands and lifted high. He accepted their adoration and simply raised his weapon over his head, savoring the chanting of his name. As he was carried and praised by the farrow he saw Dr. Arkadius standing alone in the clearing, watching. Carver inclined his head toward the other warlock in the barest nod of recognition. He saw the doctor nod back to him and knew their understanding still held. "Back to the great hall!" Lord Carver shouted. "Bring as much gator meat as you can carry! We will feast well!" Every victory must include its proper reward, and the successful defense of territory was every bit as much to be savored as the joy of conquest.

Only the shamans among them spared time for the dead. Those bodies would be collected and dealt with once meat for the feast had been gathered. Lord Carver left it to others to count the fallen, for he knew those warriors would be replaced by young hopefuls from the villages abroad who would hear his name. The glorious dream felt nearer than ever before, and Carver's eyes burned with zealous conviction. Word would spread, he knew, of this victory and his unwillingness to allow intrusion into even the least of his territories.

He had once again proven he was invincible, to Arkadius as well as to the chiefs. In time the farrow scattered across Immoren would be compelled to flock to his banner, and together they would engage in glorious conquest. They would seize lands from the arrogant humans to create their own kingdom, with Lord Carver enthroned as their king.

BUILDING A MINION ARMY

Whether as part of self-preservation or campaigns of conquest, minion pacts bind groups with mutual interests at a moment's notice to fight as an army against enemies intruding on their territories or standing in their way. Though small bands negotiate for their services from an inferior position and often endure coercion or even enslavement by greater powers, when combined they become truly formidable. Tribal rivalries are put aside as fearsome and charismatic leaders rally warriors from multiple regions under a single banner, sometimes even uniting different species within a region. These groups usually disperse to resume their infighting once the larger, external threat is dealt with.

To field a minion army, you must choose either a minion pact or a Theme Force. Each pact and Theme Force includes rules for building the army. In addition to the guidelines presented in a contract or Theme Force, minion armies follow all the normal army composition rules.

The complete rules for Theme Forces can be found in *HORDES: Primal Mk II*.

PACTS

Minion pacts detail the background of the minions' leaders, the history of the pact, and rules for constructing an army. While one player may choose a new pact each time he plays, another might dedicate himself to a particular pact, painting and modeling his forces to reflect the flavor or color scheme of a specific army.

THORNFALL ALLIANCE

Once the farrow tribes of Immoren were scattered, but recently a summit of gathered chiefs sealed an alliance in blood oaths at an old battleground called Thornfall. The greatest of those gathered, the warlord Lord Carver, cowed the rest into submitting to his violent visions of conquest. Where Lord Carver travels, lesser farrow leaders are intimidated into obedience, though their loyalty has a dubious duration. Backed by the genius of Dr. Arkadius and his surgically enhanced warbeasts, the Thornfall Alliance is poised to strike fear into the hearts of the civilized kingdoms.

ARMY COMPOSITION

- An army constructed under the Thornfall Alliance pact can include any Minion Farrow model/units.

- The army can also include Dr. Arkadius, Alten Ashley, Gudrun the Wanderer, Saxon Orrik, and Viktor Pendrake.

- Increase the FA of all non-character Farrow models and units included in the army by +1.

SPECIAL RULES

- Farrow units in this army gain Advance Deployment ⏵.

BLINDWATER CONGREGATION

The gatormen of Blindwater Lake are the core of a growing reptilian cult. Led by the ancient warrior and mystic Bloody Barnabas, this cult schemes to deliver the tide of bloodshed their master requires to fuel an apocalyptic ascension to godhood. As the pragmatic bokor Calaban guides from the shadows, gatormen from across the region assemble alongside the bog trogs and other swamp creatures subjugated into fighting alongside them.

ARMY COMPOSITION

- An army constructed under the Blindwater Congregation pact can include all minion models/units with the Amphibious ability.

- The army can also include Feralgeists, Swamp Gobber Bellows Crew, Thrullg, Totem Hunter, and Victor Pendrake.

- Increase the FA of all non-character Gatorman models and units included in the army by +1.

SPECIAL RULES

- You may place up to two 3″ AOEs anywhere completely within 20″ of the back edge of your deployment zone after terrain has been placed but before either player deploys his army. The AOEs are shallow water terrain features. AOEs cannot be placed within 3″ of another terrain feature.

DR. ARKADIUS
MAD SCIENCE

WARBEASTS
Minion Farrow
non-character warbeasts

UNITS
Farrow units

SOLOS
Farrow solos, Rorsh & Brine

TIER 1

Requirements: The army can include only the models listed above.

Benefit: Reduce the point cost of War Hog warbeasts in this army by 1.

TIER 2

Requirements: This army includes one or more Farrow Bone Grinder units.

Benefit: You can redeploy one model/unit for each Farrow Bone Grinder unit in the army after both players have deployed but before the first player's first turn. The redeployed models must be placed on the table in a location they could have been deployed initially.

TIER 3

Requirements: The army includes one or more Farrow Brigand units.

Benefit: You gain +1 on your starting roll for the game.

TIER 4

Requirements: Dr. Arkadius' battlegroup includes three or more War Hog warbeasts.

Benefit: Warbeasts in the army gain +2 SPD during your first turn of the game.

LORD CARVER, BMMD, ESQ. III
THE GOLDEN HORDE

WARBEASTS
Minion Farrow
non-character warbeasts

UNITS
Farrow units

SOLOS
Farrow solos, Rorsh & Brine

TIER 1

Requirements: The army can include only the models listed above.

Benefit: One Farrow Brigand or Farrow Razorback Crew unit gains Advance Deployment. Additionally, Farrow Brigand units in this army become FA U.

TIER 2

Requirements: The army includes Rorsh & Brine.

Benefit: Models/units in this army gain Pathfinder during your first turn of the game. Additionally, reduce the point cost of light warbeasts in Rorsh's battlegroup by 1 and reduce the point cost of heavy warbeasts in his battlegroup by 2.

TIER 3

Requirements: The army includes two or more Farrow Brigand units.

Benefit: Reduce the point cost of Farrow Brigand units by 1.

TIER 4

Requirements: Carver's battlegroup includes three or more warbeasts.

Benefit: Models in Carver's battlegroup gains gain Advance Move. (Before the start of the game but after both players have deployed, a model with Advance Move can make a full advance.)

CALABAN, THE GRAVE WALKER
BAD RELIGION

WARBEASTS
Minion Gatorman non-character warbeasts

UNITS
Bog Trog Ambushers, Farrow Bone Grinders, Gatorman units

SOLOS
Croak Hunters, Feralgeists, Gatorman solos, Wrong Eye & Snapjaw

TIER 1
Requirements: The army can include only the models listed above.

Benefit: Models / units in this army gain Stealth ⓢ during the first round of the game

TIER 2
Requirements: The army includes one or more Farrow Bone Grinder units.

Benefit: Feralgeist solos in this army gain Advance Move. (Before the start of the game but after both players have deployed, a model with Advance Move can make a full advance.)

TIER 3
Requirements: The army includes Wrong Eye & Snapjaw.

Benefit: Wrong Eye and warbeasts in his battlegroup gain Advance Deployment ⓐ. Additionally, reduce the point cost of light warbeasts in Wrong Eye's battlegroup by 1 and reduce the point cost of heavy warbeasts in his battlegroup by 2.

TIER 4
Requirements: Calaban's battlegroup includes four or more warbeasts.

Benefit: Your deployment zone is extended 2″ forward.

BLOODY BARNABAS
APEX PREDATORS

WARBEASTS
Minion Gatorman non-character warbeasts

UNITS
Bog Trog Ambushers, Gatorman units

SOLOS
Croak Hunters, Gatorman solos, Wrong Eye & Snapjaw

TIER 1
Requirements: The army can include only the models listed above.

Benefit: Gatorman Posse units become FA U.

TIER 2
Requirements: The army includes one or more Bog Trog Ambusher units.

Benefit: You gain +1 on your starting roll for the game.

TIER 3
Requirements: The army includes two or more Gatorman Posse units.

Benefit: For every two Gatorman Posse units in the army, place one 3″ AOE anywhere completely within 20″ of the back edge of Barnabas' deployment zone after terrain has been placed but before either player deploys his army. The AOE is shallow water terrain. These AOEs cannot be placed within 3″ of another terrain feature.

TIER 4
Requirements: Barnabas' battlegroup includes three or more heavy warbeasts.

Benefit: Reduce the point cost of heavy warbeasts in Barnabas' battlegroup by 1.

ALLIES OF DUBIOUS CONVENIENCE

The wilderness is a vast place, and the inhabitants of its remote stretches are as varied as the rugged landscapes. In the shadows of the great armies that now battle across the primeval forests, deserts, and plains are countless smaller, unaffiliated groups. Though many lack the sheer numbers or martial agendas of their neighbors, they have their own diverse motivations and needs. Many of those who populate the hinterlands find themselves swept up in the conflicts of the greater factions, either by choice or through force of arms. A rare few are able to bargain with the greater forces on their own terms and lend their unique talents at a price. Even these exceptional individuals must take precautions against their employers resorting to coercion.

The realities of survival in the dangerous wilds mean many smaller tribes find it virtually necessary to ally with other groups. Occasionally this arrangement develops from some other shared interest, such as long-term relationships between tribes or races. Certain tribes of farrow, for example, have lived closely enough alongside neighboring trollkin kriels that the communities share cultural ties and other commonalities that encourage them to defend and protect one another. More commonly tribes ally with one another in the face of a short-term threat, such as happened when the encroachment of Khadoran rail projects through Blackwood Forest recently spurred the indigenous gobbers and farrow to take up arms alongside the Wolves of Orboros in defense of their homes. Once the Khadoran rail crews were slaughtered the alliance dissolved, as its constituent members had no interest in further association.

Perhaps more frequently, individuals or smaller groups may find their neighbors have need of their specialized knowledge, battle experience, or unique magics. In such situations barter or promises of future services are made. Because few organizations in the wild mint or use coin, the trades are most often for food, shelter, or access to territory. These deals are only as equitable as the more powerful group cares to make them; in some cases merely a token payment is made and the minions are essentially intimidated into fighting alongside their new "allies."

Coercion and violence are by far the most common ways the unaffiliated find themselves fighting for others. The harsh necessities of life in the most dangerous parts of Immoren leave little room for sentiment and the niceties of civilization. Outright enslavement is the standard. The various farrow tribes are notorious for subjugating one another, for example.

Dealing with the factions warring on the fringes of western Immoren is risky even under the best of circumstances, but some exceptional individuals thrive in such an environment. Those who have made a reputation and who take the time to barter directly with these factions can manage mutually beneficial arrangements.

Adventurers may be motivated purely by the sport of hunting deadly beasts on the battlefield, while others are interested in exploration for its own sake. Moving across the uncharted and hostile wilderness is dangerous in the extreme, and accompanying an armed war band or military force offers a degree of protection. Gaining allies may also allow an individual to gain access to normally impassable areas and thereby gather vital intelligence on other enemies. In some cases individuals may be motivated solely by the desire to form alliances and relationships with those inhabiting the wilds.

Without long-standing codes and contracts such as those among the mercenaries of the human Iron Kingdoms, such dealings are fraught with peril. A free agent must offer his combat expertise or other skills in order to form a relationship with specific allies or contacts within the faction, and he must possess a familiarity with their methods and expectations. As in all barter, such negotiations come down to the recognition that each side can be of use to the other, combined with a certain wary respect. Free agents who serve these warring factions have to be cautious and ensure their allies have reason to leave them healthy, prosperous, and unfettered. Each faction has shown some willingness to make such arrangements.

PROTECTING THE KRIELS: THE TROLLBLOODS

The diverse kriels of the trollkin are often willing to deal with their less numerous and powerful neighbors on an equitable basis. Of the factions on the wilderness fringes the kriels have proven to be the most honorable and forthright in their dealings with outsiders. In many regions the kriels are isolated and do not recognize any formal higher authority, so dealings with one kriel will not necessarily carry over

to others. This has begun to change as kriels unite under leaders like Madrak Ironhide, Hoarluk Doomshaper, and Grissel Bloodsong, but not even arrangements with one of these leaders are always recognized by another. Some longstanding friends and proven allies, such as Professor Pendrake and Alten Ashley, have earned reputations affording them ready access to kriels across a broad region.

Due to their occasional contact with the civilized nations, the trollkin represent one of the few groups capable of paying in coin. Though by no means common, some bounty hunters, marksmen, and other adventurers have found employ with the kriels with arrangements similar to mercenary contracts. More often, individual kriels or chiefs make alliances with neighboring groups in return for mutual protection or access to food stores, fresh water, and other supplies. Arrangements for grain or shelter during the winter are common between trollkin kriels and some farrow tribes, particularly in regions where the groups face mutual threats like skorne slavers or encroaching human armies.

Not all trollkin are above intimidating others into aiding their cause. Even the most peaceful of kriels consider their kith and kin of greater import than any outsider, and when threatened some kriels will bully or intimidate others into fighting for them. Small bog trog tribes may be pressed into service by kriels in need of more warriors, particularly those fighting near marshland or other terrain where they have a great advantage. This sort of coercion can cause long-term problems, though, as those pressed into service may resent the entire kriel that used them. Both bog trogs and farrow have been known to conduct raiding campaigns on villages perceived guilty of unfair dealings. Even a large and well-defended trollkin village will suffer from having food stores repeatedly looted and sentries murdered. Wise trollkin elders see the advantages of favoring negotiation over coercion.

BOUND BY OATH AND DUTY: THE CIRCLE ORBOROS

The blackclads of the Circle Orboros count numerous tribes among their vassals and temporary allies and have cultivated relationships with almost every group that makes its home in the wilds of western Immoren. Over long centuries, the druids have carefully ingratiated themselves with those they would have serve them. In many instances, this relationship is largely one-sided: the Circle requires its "allies" to fight on its behalf as favor for services the blackclads may have performed generations earlier. The druids have a long-standing tradition of taking advantage of the religious superstitions of certain tribes, particularly those that worship the Devourer Wurm. Some of these groups see the blackclads as special emissaries of their god and therefore serve them willingly. Certain tribes may have been offered nebulous rewards for their long-term aid to the Circle and have been strung along with vague promises for centuries. The nature of these agreements varies considerably from one regional overseer or potent to the next, with some being diligent in honoring promises while others are more manipulative. Though some of the more harshly abused groups do break with the druids, most do not, as the blackclads have a fearsome reputation. Rather, tribal leaders learn to be more careful regarding their future agreements.

Even their oldest allies are ultimately considered disposable weapons in the organization's arsenal. When need be, the druids do not shy from openly intimidating or forcing others to do their bidding, and those individuals who choose to work for the Circle on a short-term basis

typically understand they will be considered expendable combatants. Still, the Circle can offer much to those capable of effectively exploiting their talents. They possess a deep knowledge of some of the fundamental secrets of the world and may be willing to share their less tightly guarded knowledge in return for valuable services. While the druids are sometimes reluctant to pay their debts, they are willing to lend their strength to preserve those allies that have served them well. For isolated villages or tribes, such arrangements can provide protection from more powerful and hostile neighbors. Druids occasionally provide supernatural assistance such as increasing crops, driving away dangerous predators, encouraging hunting game to repopulate a barren area, or diverting a stream to provide water for allies suffering from drought.

SLAVERS OF THE EAST: THE SKORNE

The skorne largely prefer to dispense with the niceties of bargain and alliance altogether, simply enslaving any they do not put to the sword. Since their arrival, the skorne have subjugated countless tribes of farrow, gatormen, and others. Those they defeat fall under the yoke of the Skorne Empire and are utilized as labor and fodder in their ongoing war of conquest. Members of almost every race, tribe, and species inhabiting the continent have served in bondage under the whips of the Paingiver caste. As the armies of the invading skorne have been stretched thin, they have increasingly relied on slaves to fill deficiencies in their strength of arms.

Some individuals possessing extraordinary qualities are able to strike deals with the skorne. This is more likely to happen among those skorne cohorts at the limits of the empire's influence who require the aid of local inhabitants with specialized knowledge. The leading officers of the Army of the Western Reaches have learned to rely on certain individuals like the ex-Cygnaran ranger Saxon Orrik. Orrik proved his credibility and skill by guiding the army across the Bloodstone Desert and remains an invaluable local contact and scout. Being human he will never be fully trusted, but his knowledge of the local region and his insight into the workings of human armies have earned him the ear of many high-ranking skorne. Orrik managed to weather the overthrow of Vinter Raelthorne with his arrangements intact, and it is not uncommon for other individuals who wish to find work with the skorne to seek him out as an intermediary, an arrangement that suits him perfectly.

COMPELLED BY THE DRAGON: THE LEGION OF EVERBLIGHT

The Legion of Everblight has no need of alliances with outsiders. What it needs, it takes, pressing the strong into service and bleeding the weak out to fuel the production of ever-greater numbers of spawn. Even those who live long enough to be forced into fighting for the Legion are almost invariably later sacrificed and their blood used to fill the Legion's nightmarish spawning vessels. The small number who prove useful may be spared, but given the harsh pace the Legion keeps and the poor shelter and sustenance made available to slaves, few minions survive lengthy campaigns. Exceptions are rare, and such allies of convenience could well be abandoned or murdered the moment Everblight deems it prudent.

The majority who do endure in their captivity find themselves at the bottom of the Legion's nascent hierarchy. As time goes on, prolonged exposure to the dragon's blighted servants and warlocks may begin to warp them in both body and mind. Though this second-hand blighting does not provide the benefits of the dragon's deliberate manipulation, it often twists the flesh of those it touches. It is not uncommon for those enslaved by the Legion to slowly develop the scales, spiked growths, and talons the blighted Nyss and ogrun are proud to bear. The Legion's soldiers are more accepting and lenient with those who bear these blighted marks, and those so marred realize that even if they could escape the Legion's grasp they would have nowhere to go. Their bodies are already the dragon's, and their souls are not long to follow.

Despite the often callous disregard the greater factions have for their allied tribes, slaves, or hired swords, minions bring substantial benefits to those they aid. Their weapons and tactics can be extremely potent when properly wielded, and even the most seemingly insignificant individuals can tip the balance of power.

FERALGEIST
MINION SOLO

The wild itself has desires that are not easily deterred, not even by death.

—Morvahna the Autumnblade

FERALGEIST						
SPD	STR	MAT	RAT	DEF	ARM	CMD
6	0	3	0	14	11	8

FIELD ALLOWANCE	3
POINT COST	1
SMALL BASE	

Minion – This model will work for Circle, Legion, Skorne, and Trollbloods.

FERALGEIST

Incorporeal

Undead

Spiritbind – When a living warbeast in this model's command range is destroyed but not removed from play by an attack, this model can bind itself to the beast. If more than one eligible model attempts to bind to the warbeast, the closest model binds to it. If this model binds itself to the warbeast, the warbeast remains on the table and you take control of it. Remove this model from the table and remove all fury points on the warbeast. Any effects, spells, or animi on this model expire when it is removed. The warbeast becomes a friendly Minion, gains Undead , and no longer belongs to a battlegroup. Remove 1 damage point from each of the warbeast's aspects. The warbeast cannot activate the turn Spiritbind is used, cannot be forced or healed, and loses its animus. This model can exit the warbeast during your Maintenance Phase. If it does, place this model completely within 3˝ of the warbeast, then the warbeast is destroyed. If the warbeast is destroyed or removed from play while this model is bound to it, this model is forced to exit the warbeast.

Feralgeists lurk in the shadows of the deep forest, their ghostly, greenish forms drifting easily through trees and stones toward the scent of imminent death. As insubstantial as breath, these spectral entities hunger to inhabit flesh and walk for a time as other creatures do. But because they are unable to control living bodies, they instead descend into the carcasses of freshly slain beasts to reanimate them in a semblance of life. Each of these bodies responds to their will and lumbers to its feet with empty, hollow eyes. Feralgeists in such a guise pose a deadly threat to any who venture near, lashing out with the claws or fangs of the corpses they inhabit. Still, these formidable puppet masters cannot create life from death; as their flimsy, borrowed bodies crumble from decay, the feralgeists are soon forced to seek new hosts.

Most who have seen these wraiths have presumed they are what they seem: ghosts haunting the forest. The wilderness masters of Orboros, however, claim feralgeists are naturally occurring spirits drawn to death despite never having been alive. They are vengeful manifestations of nature that strike against intruders or interlopers in wild places. These cunning and patient creatures haunt the fringes of battles or follow warbeasts as they march to war, as though they can sense the violence to come and the vessels they will soon inhabit. The very aspect that compels feralgeists to dead beasts and grants them control over corpses also makes them vulnerable to warlocks, who through force of will can bind these spirits into service.

Their hunger for the arcane is insatiable. I've seen one tear apart a warjack just to consume the mechanikal components.
—Viktor Pendrake

TACTICAL TIPS

ARCANE INTERFERENCE – If the model hit is part of a unit, upkeep spells and animi on that unit also expire.

SPELL WARD – This model is shielded from friendly and enemy spells alike.

The scholars of the Iron Kingdoms have long known of the terrible thrullgs, extremely rare creatures that exist on a diet of mechanika and sorcery. Though these creatures generally seem to prefer lurking in the sewers of urban areas, they have been seen in growing numbers on the far-flung battlefields of western Immoren. As the hidden wars between the factions of the hinterlands escalate, thrullgs are increasingly lured from their hiding places to be used as dangerous living weapons.

Minion – This model will work for Circle, Legion, Skorne, and Trollbloods.

THRULLG

▶ **Advance Deployment**

✠ **Fearless**

Arcane Interference – When this model hits another model with an attack, upkeep spells and animi on the model hit expire and it loses the focus points on it. When this model hits a warjack with an attack, that warjack suffers Disruption. (A warjack suffering Disruption loses its focus points and cannot be allocated focus or channel spells for one round.)

Arcane Consumption – When an enemy model casts a spell or uses an animus while in this model's command range, after the spell is cast the enemy model suffers 1 damage point and this model heals 1 damage point.

Spell Ward – This model cannot be targeted by spells.

CLAW

⊘ **Magical Weapon**

TENTACLES

⊘ **Magical Weapon**

↗ **Reach**

THRULLG						
SPD	STR	MAT	RAT	DEF	ARM	CMD
6	9	7	1	13	16	7

CLAW	
POW	P+S
3	12

TENTACLES	
POW	P+S
4	13

DAMAGE	8
FIELD ALLOWANCE	2
POINT COST	3
MEDIUM BASE	

Vicious and unpredictable, thrullgs cannot be tamed or controlled. They must be baited to the battlefield with arcane trinkets or the scent of sorcery, then unleashed upon the warlocks, arcanists, and warjacks of the enemy. Such combatants are irresistible prey to the creatures' supernormal senses.

Even a single thrullg is a valuable asset to any army willing to risk its predations, as it will invariably seek out the most powerful of the enemy's arcanists with a gnawing and unrelenting hunger. When it finds and defeats its prey, it wraps powerful tentacles about the victim and sucks the essence of his occult powers from him even as its claws sink deep into his flesh. Its very presence saps arcane strength from those nearby, inflicting a terrible agony on its favored prey.

ALTEN ASHLEY
MERCENARY MINION CHARACTER SOLO

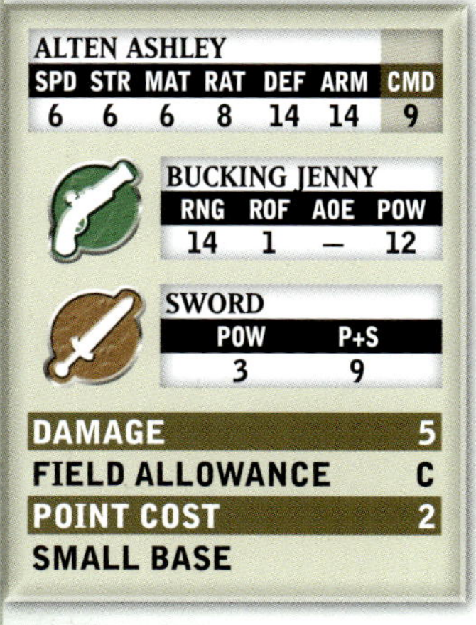

ALTEN ASHLEY						
SPD	STR	MAT	RAT	DEF	ARM	CMD
6	6	6	8	14	14	9

BUCKING JENNY			
RNG	ROF	AOE	POW
14	1	—	12

SWORD	
POW	P+S
3	9

DAMAGE	5
FIELD ALLOWANCE	C
POINT COST	2
SMALL BASE	

Mercenary – This model will work for Cygnar, Khador, and the Protectorate.

Minion – This model will work for Circle and Trollbloods.

ALTEN ASHLEY

- **Advance Deployment**

- **Pathfinder**

Camouflage – This model gains an additional +2 DEF when benefiting from concealment or cover.

Monster Hunter – When this model hits a warbeast with an attack, the warbeast suffers d6 points of damage to a branch of your choice.

Swift Hunter – When this model destroys an enemy model with a normal ranged attack, immediately after the attack is resolved it can advance up to 2″.

TACTICAL TIPS

Camouflage – If a model ignores concealment or cover, it also ignores concealment or cover's Camouflage bonus.

Monster Hunter – Apply this damage before the damage roll.

Some men are just rugged through and through: mean as a gorax, born with an eagle's eye, and possessed of such irrepressible gumption they become legends in their own time—or at least in their own minds. Alten Ashley is such a man. Unlike some braggarts, though, he lives up to his reputation as an exceptional hunter of the great beasts that stalk the wilds of western Immoren. Most men feel fear at the emergence of previously hidden enemies and the onset of war, but not Alten Ashley. For him these conflicts hold the thrilling promise of both gold and danger.

Ashley's jealous detractors dismiss him as a money-grubbing mercenary, but wealth is the least of his motivators. Though he appreciates a healthy purse—and his vast skill certainly commands a fair fee—the thrill of taking down Caen's most dangerous creatures is what truly drives him. Alten gleefully embraces the peculiar madness that demands some men seek danger instead of turning from it. Neither the reward nor the kill matters to him as much as the excitement of the hunt and the gathering of esoteric monster lore.

Ashley does not speak of a homeland, but his accent marks his roots as being somewhere on the western coast of Cygnar. For sport or hire he has traveled more than most; he has tales of tracking one of Blighterghast's dragonspawn deep in the Wyrmwall Mountains, narrowly escaping a rampaging dire troll in the Gnarls, and hunting the largest frost drake ever recorded in the frozen wastes of Khador. Deciding the cold did not suit him, he swung through the

Thornwood Forest killing warpwolves before making his way to the fringes of the Bloodstone Marches. The only place he is seen with any regularity is the Sanity's Bastion saloon in the dusty no-man's-land of a town called Ternon Crag, some fifty miles east of Cygnar.

With a reputation for being so boisterous as to be considered obnoxious, Alten has earned few true friends. He is nevertheless respected by both Kossite woodsmen and Morridane scouts. Even the Widowmakers grudgingly acknowledge Ashley's shooting skill, despite his lack of formal training.

The hunter's truly monstrous rifle, named Bucking Jenny, has a thick, large-bored barrel designed to blast open the thickest hides. The weapon can punch a hole through a man as if he weren't there, and its bipod allows Alten to aim more accurately while hiding prone in the underbrush. Though Ashley relies heavily on this oversized gun, he is proficient enough with a sword to hold his own when a target closes to tear him apart.

Ashley will be the first to insist it is not his weapons that make him deadly but rather his experience and knowledge. The monster hunter has already fought more dangerous creatures than a Nyss ranger might face in a century. He knows their habits, their strengths, and their weak points— exactly where to shoot in order to deflate a dire troll's lung, for example. Not many living creatures can survive a few rounds from Alten's rifle, and he's just as capable of slipping a blade between a beast's ribs to tickle its heart. Spurning the easy life, Ashley seeks out one dangerous challenge after another. Somehow he always manages to escape unscathed and with more experience, more coin, and more stories.

BRUN CRAGBACK & LUG
RHULIC MERCENARY MINION CHARACTER SOLO & MERCENARY MINION CHARACTER HEAVY WARBEAST

The Glass Peaks are cold, unforgiving, and treacherous. Anyone who feels at home alone up there is liable to be the same.

—Decklin Steelthunder, Searforge Commission officer

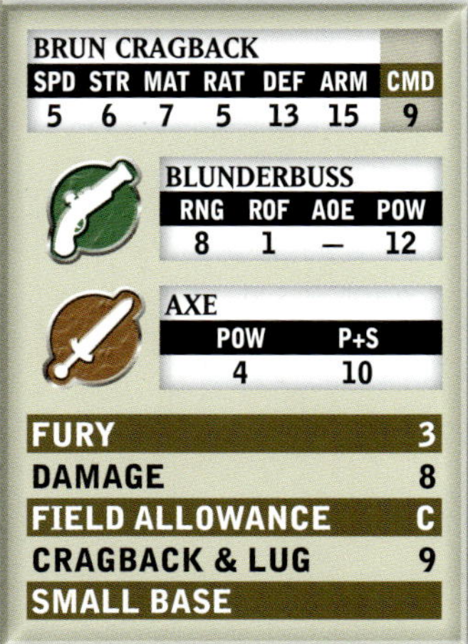

BRUN CRAGBACK						
SPD	STR	MAT	RAT	DEF	ARM	CMD
5	6	7	5	13	15	9

BLUNDERBUSS			
RNG	ROF	AOE	POW
8	1	—	12

AXE	
POW	P+S
4	10

FURY	3
DAMAGE	8
FIELD ALLOWANCE	C
CRAGBACK & LUG	9
SMALL BASE	

Mercenaries – These models will work for Searforge Commission.

Minions – These models will work for Circle and Trollbloods.

BRUN CRAGBACK

✠ **Fearless**

❄ **Immunity: Cold**

🐾 **Pathfinder**

Flank [Lug] – When this model makes a melee attack against an enemy model within the melee range of a friendly model of the type indicated, this model gains +2 to attack rolls and gains an additional damage die.

Lesser Warlock – This model is not a warlock but has the following warlock special rules: Battlegroup Commander, Control Area, Damage Transference, Forcing, Fury Manipulation, Healing, and Spellcaster.

Lifebond [Lug] – While B2B with Lug, this model can transfer damage to Lug without spending fury.

Limited Battlegroup – The only warbeast that can be in this model's battlegroup is Lug.

SPELLS	COST	RNG	AOE	POW	UP	OFF
STONEHOLD	2	SELF	–	–	YES	NO

Enemy models roll one less die on attack damage rolls against this model. This model and friendly models B2B with it cannot be knocked down.

TACTICAL TIPS

LESSER WARLOCK – This model's type is solo, not warlock.

kinfolk and under cover of a moonless night, Brun marched straight into the human camp with his axe in hand. His disdain for the humans grew even greater when he saw they had not even bothered to post sentries. The ensuing carnage was almost too easy, hardly a sporting test of his skill. When he returned to his kinsmen soaked in gore, he was surprised to see horror on their faces and hear their protests that he had gone too far. Fearful their clan would bear the brunt of his impropriety if the Moot decided to get involved, they talked of exiling him and stripping him of his clan name. Brun refused to wait for their decision. Before they could ask him to leave he turned his back on them, eager to find his destiny alone among the mountains.

The only activity Brun enjoys more than a good brawl is exploring unknown territory. Unlike most of his kin he has never felt the urge to settle in one specific place. As soon as the dwarf feels he has mastered every nook and cranny of a given locale, he packs up his tent and travels on. He has vowed never to own any more than he and his pack mule can carry, and when necessary he has abandoned even that without hesitation. He perfectly remembers every location he has ever visited, as if each footstep inscribes the peaks and valleys he walks directly onto the map in his mind.

This compulsion to venture into new territory has taken Brun to the frozen regions of Khador, northern Llael, and Cygnar's Wyrmwall Mountains. He has never lacked for work as a guide or battle-ready escort, providing assistance to those traveling from one place to another in hostile regions. He does not work regularly as a mercenary— at least not as often as those who earn their coin as seasonal soldiers—but he accepts periodic work with the Searforge Commission when his supplies or funds run low. Because he prefers to avoid any type of sizable community, Searforge agents

A rugged and fearless loner with intimate knowledge of every game trail and mountain pass in western Immoren, Brun Cragback first earned notoriety in the remote regions along the periphery of Rhul. He is a seasoned warrior who would rather kill a man than endure a lengthy conversation. When blood needs spilling, it is far better to have Brun as an ally than face him in battle. With his gun or axe in hand and Lug beside him, he fears no man or beast.

Before becoming a recluse, Brun Cragback served his small dwarven clan by patrolling the western peaks near the border with Khador. His kin were embroiled in a feud with Khadoran settlers of Skirov descent who regularly trespassed in their territory. Given the nature of the twisting mountain passes, it was difficult to say where Khador ended and Rhul began, which had given rise to intermittent conflict for decades. These skirmishes were generally small and inconsequential, considered an almost respectable tradition by many.

Not a dwarf who appreciates half-measures, Brun decided to settle matters once and for all. Without consulting his

sometimes have to track him down in order to arrange for his services. Given the difficulty in separating him from his oversized bear companion (and the scarcity of baths in the wild), Brun's avoidance of towns is likely appreciated.

Brun has spent time with some of the northern trollkin kriels and has contacts among the human blackclads who call themselves the Circle. When he finds himself near erupting conflict, he stands ready to leap into the fray with pragmatic efficiency. Accompanied by his gigantic bear Lug, he inflicts a heavy toll on any enemy he meets; for potential employers, enduring his sour disposition seems a small price to pay for such ferocity.

Brun earned a name for himself through his own skill with arms, but without question the enormous armored bear that tags along with him enhances his reputation tenfold. Few sights are more

terrifying than a giant, exuberant bear rearing up on its hind legs to let loose an ear-shattering roar before charging to attack. Those who face the mass of fur and muscle do not have time to consider its mood before claws rip them in half. What would surprise such victims is that Lug is not truly filled with murderous intent, being a generally good-natured, simple-minded beast that merely likes to play rough.

Brun Cragback did not need to coerce, train, or pressure Lug into fighting. Rather, the bear takes delight in romping through masses of men and swatting at everything within reach of his massive claws. Clearly the bear has no real sense of mortality; in fact, Lug is relatively oblivious to his own injuries in battle so long as he is given free reign to play. The only hint of sorrow the bear demonstrates is after the fighting, when he paws forlornly at the fallen bodies as if urging them to stand up and play some more.

Brun claims not to know how long he and Lug have been together, but he reckons it to be less than a decade. Though he does not often wax nostalgic telling stories about Lug, Brun relishes the tale of how he and the bear came to travel together. He encountered a white mountain bear while hunting near Nyss territory in the Shard Spires. Eager to acquire a nice, thick fur pelt before the coming winter, Brun shot down the ornery bear without a second thought. He was in the middle of the messy business of skinning her when he heard a querulous roar and the sound of approaching paws. In a moment of unexplained inspiration, Brun wrapped himself in the hide and stood to confront the newcomer.

Rounding the mountain pass was a half-grown but already dangerous adolescent bear—apparently the dead animal's cub—which slid to a confused stop in front of him and suspiciously sniffed the hide he was wearing. At last the bear sat back on its haunches, accepted some of Brun's food, and tucked in. Lug has since followed Brun Cragback's every footstep. Convinced the stupid bear thinks he is its mother, Brun has continued to wear the improvised cloak. Whether Lug would actually cease to recognize him without the hide seems unlikely, but the dwarf maintains he'd rather err on the side of caution.

ANIMUS	COST	RNG	AOE	POW	UP	OFF
BEAR HANDS	1	SELF	–	–	NO	NO

When this model hits an enemy model with a normal melee attack, it can choose to knock down the enemy model or push it 3" directly away. Bear Hands lasts for one turn.

Though Brun regularly hurls every foul epithet imaginable at his animal companion, the bond between them is obvious. Brun claims Lug is the dimmest bear ever born, but outsiders watching the beast have seen it demonstrate undeniable cunning. Belying his casual attitude, the dwarf has spent a sizable portion of his mercenary earnings outfitting Lug for war. Brun purchased special plated barding at no small expense from a master smith out of Skirov, and the bear seems to take pride in wearing it. Brun generally armors the bear only when he expects battle, and the beast becomes unaccountably excited as Brun straps each plate to his bulk. Those who have seen them after battle confirm Brun always feeds Lug first, even when provisions are short the dwarf himself goes hungry. Cragback claims this is simply a matter of self-preservation, denying his actions are any sign of affection for the smelly beast.

Together Brun and Lug walk into the path of gunfire, frenzying trolls, or charging pikemen with equally casual disregard. Brun brushes aside questions about Lug, claiming he has no idea why the "confounded animal" follows him. Whatever the reason, their raw destructive power is undeniable. The pair has fought Khadoran soldiers; Nyss warriors ("with scales and without"); and a wide assortment of bandits, outcasts, and bloodthirsty monsters. Recently they traveled farther south into the Cygnaran mountains after hiring on with Searforge to escort supply shipments. This was a grueling ordeal requiring the pair to battle through war-torn regions in both Llael and the Thornwood before reaching the remote dwarven conclaves at Orven and Ironhead in Cygnar. In the process of this journey they also renewed contact with trollkin kriels in the Wyrmwall region and sent feelers to druids of the Circle Orboros to let the blackclads know they are looking for paying work. Nothing fazes Brun Cragback. Whether it flies, slithers, or breathes fire, he will gladly shoot it, chop it down, or send Lug to crush it.

LUG

Immunity: Cold

Pathfinder

Companion [Brun Cragback] – This model is included in any army that includes Brun Cragback. If Cragback is destroyed or removed from play, remove this model from play. This model is part of Cragback's battlegroup.

Flank [Brun Cragback] – When this model makes a melee attack against an enemy model within the melee range of a friendly model of the type indicated, this model gains +2 to attack rolls and gains an additional damage die.

Warbeast Bond [Brun Cragback] – This model is bonded to Brun Cragback. While it is within 3" of Cragback and is not stationary, Cragback cannot be targeted by free strikes and gains +2 DEF against melee attacks, and models do not gain back strike bonuses while attacking Cragback.

CLAW

Open Fist

Chain Attack: Grab & Smash – If this model hits the same model with both its initial attacks with this weapon, after resolving the attacks it can immediately make a double-hand throw, head-butt, headlock/weapon lock, push, or throw power attack against that target.

LUG						
SPD	STR	MAT	RAT	DEF	ARM	CMD
5	12	5	1	12	18	6

CLAW	POW	P+S
L	3	15

CLAW	POW	P+S
R	3	15

FURY	4
THRESHOLD	9
FIELD ALLOWANCE	C
LARGE BASE	

GUDRUN THE WANDERER
MERCENARY MINION OGRUN CHARACTER SOLO

Try to kill me if you want, but you had better make sure it sticks. Death spits me back into the world each time.

—Gudrun the Wanderer

GUDRUN						
SPD	STR	MAT	RAT	DEF	ARM	CMD
6	9	7	4	13	15	9

BATTLE GLAIVE		
	POW	P+S
	6	15

DAMAGE	8
FIELD ALLOWANCE	C
POINT COST	3

MEDIUM BASE

Mercenary – This model will work for Cryx, Cygnar, and Khador.

Minion – This model will work for Circle, Legion, Skorne, and Trollbloods.

GUDRUN

◉ Advance Deployment

✪ Fearless

☾ Pathfinder

Berserk – When this model destroys one or more models with a melee attack during its combat action, immediately after the attack is resolved it must make one additional melee attack against another model in its melee range.

Binge Drinking – Once per game during its activation, this model can use Binge Drinking. This model is knocked down.

Feign Death – This model cannot be targeted by ranged or magic attacks while knocked down.

Hangover – The first time this model is disabled by an enemy attack, it heals all damage and is knocked down.

BATTLE GLAIVE

◑ Reach

An oath taken incautiously can become a curse. Gudrun the Wanderer knows this only too well, as he is able to trace all the dark twists of his destiny to a single oath given when he was too young to know better. Years have washed away his pride and self-worth, leaving behind only a tide of blood. Screams echo in his dreams and bleed into his waking life, where he sometimes still hears his victims pleading for their lives. Seeking to escape these reminders, he regularly slips into a drunken haze. He strides into battle reeking of alcohol, hood pulled down over bloodshot eyes, gripping the haft of his weapon.

Swaying unsteadily atop a rise, to some Gudrun may seem too drunk to fight as he once did. All such doubt vanishes when he steps into melee, where he leverages his massive pole arm with enough force to sunder men in half. His victims see only emptiness, not triumph, in his face; Gudrun unleashes his emotions only in the unquenchable berserker rage that sometimes consumes him. Those who have stood at his side at such times say he fights as if inviting death to come.

Gudrun learned to fight among the ogrun of his village in the Glass Peaks, watched over by the nearby Rhulic clans. Unlike the other youths, he did not spend long years traveling and testing his skills as a *bokur* before choosing a *korune*, or lord to serve. Gudrun was impatient and longed to put aside his adolescence. He sought out dwarven Clan Lord Galos Hegord, of whom the ogrun of his village spoke in hushed tones. Hegord held sway over nearby clans, boasted the finest weapons and armor, and had amassed great wealth. Gudrun swore himself to this lord, declaring him korune. Had Gudrun asked more questions, perhaps he would have discovered the dwarf's dark penchant for engaging in bloody feuds.

Hegord had long contemplated the extinction of the eastern Sigvar clan, so bad was the blood between them. Ignoring all laws of the Moot of the Hundred Houses and the sacred Edicts of the Codex, Hegord led a night raid against his rivals that quickly became wholesale extermination. Gudrun fought at his side, powerless to do anything other than obey the commands of his sworn lord. His blade murdered the innocent and young alongside the outnumbered warriors of Clan Sigvar. Blood flowed in a river down the mountain.

Clan Hegord became outlaw at once, and a host of the Mootguard set out to quash their line. Galos and most of his followers died in the battles that followed. Gudrun numbered among those few spared because the Moot Judges knew the ogrun was bound to obey his korune. They branded Gudrun's head and exiled him from Rhul forever. Some say the deaths on his hands have left a cursed legacy that shadows him wherever he goes, forbidding him from escaping his guilt by the sweet release of death.

Now he wanders, at home nowhere, drinking to oblivion while selling his services to any who will pay him to deal death. He enters any fray without discrimination, as though seeking his own destruction, and endures blows that should kill him twice over—yet still he walks. Gudrun shambles from one battlefield to the next guzzling from the jug at his waist. A self-labeled disgrace who often falls into a drunken stupor in the midst of battle, Gudrun the Wanderer nevertheless remains a skilled and valuable killer.

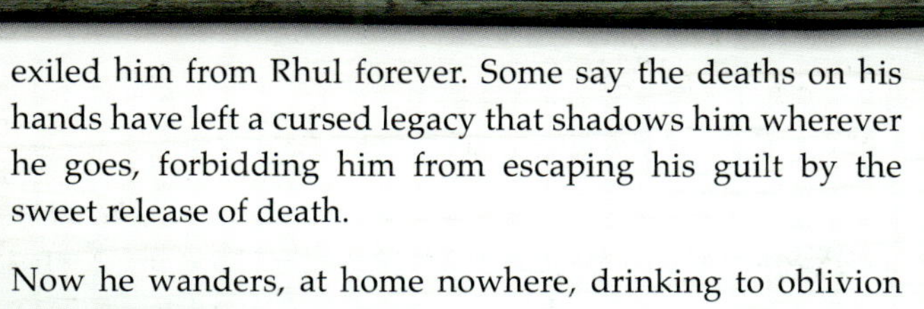

DAHLIA HALLYR & SKARATH

MERCENARY MINION CHARACTER SOLO & MERCENARY MINION TATZYLWURM CHARACTER HEAVY WARBEAST

There is a melody underlying every force, thought, and action. By playing the proper notes one can change the world.

—Dahlia Hallyr

DAHLIA HALLYR						
SPD	STR	MAT	RAT	DEF	ARM	CMD
6	4	5	4	16	12	8

FURY	4
DAMAGE	8
FIELD ALLOWANCE	C
HALLYR & SKARATH	9
SMALL BASE	

Mercenaries – These models will work for Retribution.

Minions – These models will work for Circle and Trollbloods.

DAHLIA HALLYR

✠ **Fearless**

Charmer – When a friendly warbeast frenzies in this model's control area, the warbeast can forfeit its activation.

Lesser Warlock – This model is not a warlock but has the following warlock special rules: Battlegroup Commander, Control Area, Damage Transference, Forcing, Fury Manipulation, Healing, and Spellcaster.

Limited Battlegroup – The only warbeast that can be in this model's battlegroup is Skarath.

SPELLS	COST	RNG	AOE	POW	UP	OFF
HAUNTING MELODY	2	SELF	CTRL	–	YES	NO

While in this model's control area, living enemy models cannot give or receive orders and cannot make melee or ranged attacks targeting this model.

| MIST WALKER | 2 | 6 | – | – | NO | NO |

Target model in this model's battlegroup gains Pathfinder ⟁ and Prowl for one round. (Models with Prowl gain Stealth ⊕ while within terrain that provides concealment, the AOE of a spell that provides concealment, or the AOE of a cloud effect.)

TACTICAL TIPS

LESSER WARLOCK – This model's type is solo, not warlock.

An undeniable aura of mystery surrounds all elves, whatever their background. But even among those elusive people, Dahlia Hallyr is an enigma. Though born in Ios, she has been an outsider to her own people for many decades, traveling across Immoren and refusing to settle permanently in any one place. The blood of this mysterious wanderer flows with the power of sorcery, which manifests in her singularly unearthly music. By the notes of her flute she entrances all those who hear her.

The Hallyr line traces directly back to the lost Empire of Lyoss, before the split between those who would follow Aeric to become the Nyss and those who remained in Ios. Even today, both peoples recognize the sorcerous mystique of the Hallyr name. Raised in the city of Iryss by affluent parents, Dahlia proved to be exceptional from a young age, not only for her talent but also for her stubborn refusal to heed the dictates of her elders. Her fascination with music was not atypical of her family, whose sorcery often goes hand-in-hand with artistic pursuits, but Dahlia confounded all tutors assigned to discipline her talents. She was prone to ignoring their instructions entirely, walking away mid-lesson or conducting conversations with empty air. Such behavior prompted rumors she might have inherited the less-esteemed legacy of the Hallyr line: a penchant for eccentricity verging on insanity.

A market for talented artists exists among the aristocracy living in Iryss and Shyrr. The more militant Iosans deem such circles to be decadently oblivious to the dangers facing their race, but others prefer to divert their minds through idle entertainment. Certainly Dahlia could have pursued a lucrative career helping them ignore their fate with her seductive melodies, but she again baffled her family by eschewing elven society entirely and leaving Ios, determined to pursue her own destiny. Her goals since leaving her homeland are unknown. She keeps no counsel and claims few friends. The only constant in her life has been an inner compulsion to wander and perfect her music.

Little in Dahlia's upbringing suggested she would be able to endure the vast and terrifying wilds of Immoren. Despite her apparent shortcomings, however, she has proven to be a survivor of considerable skill. Certainly the sorcerous power of her music has played a large role in keeping her safe. Some people are touched by a special sort of madness that preserves them in the face of turmoil and strife, and that seems to be true of Dahlia Hallyr.

She has shown no aversion to violence or warfare; indeed, she sometimes goes out of her way to seek it out, though she sees herself as more of an observer than a warrior. Everything she witnesses lends texture to her compositions. At times it seems as though she does not interact with the world at all but only watches from the outside.

For years Dahlia has used her entrancing music to gather guardians to help deflect the many dangers of western Immoren, and she is particularly fond of the tremendous tatzylwurms. Possessing singular grace and deadly combat prowess, these serpentine creatures respond as if born to heed the notes of her flute. Dahlia considers battle to be akin to a dance, and she enjoys the interplay of blade and serpent, as if each encounter were a performance for her eyes alone. Upon witnessing her trancelike delight in these deadly

engagements, some have come away convinced of her mental instability, but she insists these fools simply do not understand her vision of the world.

The tatzylwurm Skarath has been with her for seven years, and in that time the two have developed a refined connection that allows them to respond to one another in perfect harmony. She clearly holds this particular guardian in special esteem, speaking to it in loving tones and sometimes performing her music just for the sake of observing its graceful and sinuous dance. She can be an indulgent mistress, not always inclined to prevent the serpent from striking at prey—even if that prey is an innocent passer-by. Indeed, Dahlia sometimes restrains the serpent from consuming its meal so that its paralyzed victim can serve as a captive audience to her latest musical innovation.

To its victims Skarath is a serpentine horror, and often the last sight they see is the gape of its maw seconds before it consumes them whole. Skarath is a particularly large pale tatzylwurm, a refined specimen that perfectly embodies the cunning and savagery of its species. Tatzylwurms are among the most frightening examples of monstrous predators in western Immoren, and Skarath lives up to this pedigree. Though all tatzylwurms are dangerous, the pale variety is the most aggressive and the most inclined to use its tremendous leaping ability to pounce on anything

ANIMUS	COST	RNG	AOE	POW	UP	OFF
SERPENT STRIKE	1	6	–	–	NO	NO

Target friendly model gains Riposte. Serpent Strike lasts for one round. After the affected model makes a Riposte attack, Serpent Strike expires. (When a model with Riposte is missed by an enemy melee attack, immediately after the attack is resolved it can make one normal melee attack against the attacking model.)

it deems to be a threat, even if not motivated by hunger. Even otherwise fearless trolls steer clear of pale tatzylwurm territories. Their poison paralyzes their prey and their acid can melt flesh, allowing them to consume and digest their victims at leisure. In fact, pale tatzylwurms prefer to digest their prey alive—a process that can take several long, agonizing hours.

In her travels Dahlia has made her services available to several groups, loaning both her power and the killing prowess of Skarath to their battles. She appears to have made arrangements with members of the Circle Orboros and several large trollkin kriels in exchange for safe passage across their territories. She has visited individual Circle leaders and trollkin elders in private council. She claims no love for the urban centers of mankind and has expressed a strong loathing for the discordant hum of human magic, which jars her senses like shattering glass. She has shown no moral qualms about fighting for causes not her own, though she clearly prefers to let her serpentine companion do the dirty work. Whether her involvement in the wars that grip western Immoren is part of some more systematic plan or she is simply following the impulses of the moment is something only Dahlia knows. Certain arcanists serving the Retribution are convinced her latent power has not awakened to its full strength, and it seems clear they hope to make use of her in the wars to come.

SKARATH

Companion [Dahlia Hallyr] – This model is included in any army that includes Dahlia Hallyr. If Hallyr is destroyed or removed from play, remove this model from play. This model is part of Hallyr's battlegroup.

Serpentine – This model cannot make slam or trample power attacks and cannot be knocked down.

Warbeast Bond [Dahlia Hallyr] – This model is bonded to Dahlia Hallyr. When this model frenzies in Hallyr's control range, you choose the frenzy target.

ACID SPRAY

Continuous Effect: Corrosion

Damage Type: Corrosion

BITE

Reach

Critical Consume – On a critical hit, if the attack hit a small-based non-warlock/warcaster model the model hit is removed from play.

SAXON ORRIK
MERCENARY MINION CHARACTER SOLO

There is no truth in nature that a man cannot find within himself. Nature exists to be conquered, not studied.

—Saxon Orrik

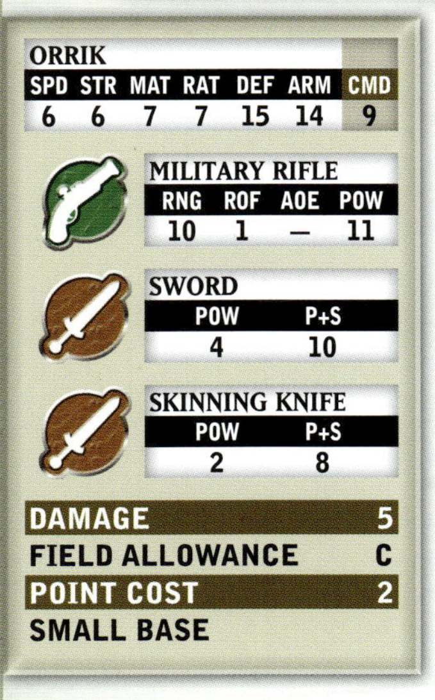

ORRIK						
SPD	STR	MAT	RAT	DEF	ARM	CMD
6	6	7	7	15	14	9

MILITARY RIFLE

RNG	ROF	AOE	POW
10	1	—	11

SWORD

POW	P+S
4	10

SKINNING KNIFE

POW	P+S
2	8

DAMAGE	5
FIELD ALLOWANCE	C
POINT COST	2
SMALL BASE	

Mercenary – This model will work for Cryx, Khador, the Protectorate.

Minion – This model will work for Circle, Skorne, and Trollbloods.

ORRIK

- Advance Deployment
- Fearless
- Pathfinder
- Stealth

Blind Spot – When an enemy warbeast misses this model with a melee attack, immediately after the attack is resolved this model can make one normal melee attack against the warbeast.

Dismember – When this model hits a warbeast with a melee attack, roll an additional damage die.

Reconnaissance (★Action) – RNG 5. Target friendly warrior model/unit. If the model/unit is in range, it gains Pathfinder for one turn.

Take Down – Models disabled by a melee attack made by this model cannot make a Tough roll. Models boxed by a melee attack made by this model are removed from play.

SKINNING KNIFE

Inflict Pain – When it hits a warbeast with this weapon, this model can place 1 fury point on or remove 1 fury point from the warbeast.

Saxon Orrik's savage cruelty is as legendary as his mastery of the wilds. He has spent his life stalking wilderness regions where mankind finds no welcome. His experiences have long since toughened him to life's misfortunes and made him callous to pain and suffering. He sees humans as no more deserving of special consideration than any animal caught in a trap or hunted to ground. Long years spent in the unforgiving desert with no company but the skorne have reinforced this attitude.

Orrik began his military career as a Cygnaran scout during the last years of the reign of Vinter Raelthorne III. His grim efficiency soon earned him the friendship of Cygnar's bloodthirsty heir, Prince Vinter IV. Orrik spent several long months serving as a ranger under the younger Vinter along the northern border, where they discovered they shared a certain cold pragmatism.

Saxon's formal military career ended abruptly after he and mercenary irregulars under his command "made an example" of several hundred Khadoran villagers who had settled too close to Cygnaran soil. A young ranger named Viktor Pendrake felt morally obligated to report his mentor's crimes to his superiors. The incident quickly escalated into a political embarrassment.

Though Vinter III was a harsh king to his subjects, he demanded strict adherence to the law, which explicitly forbade the deliberate slaughter of civilians. When word of this incident reached the king he was obliged to act. As part of a larger series of reforms and investigations, Orrik was dishonorably discharged and sentenced to twenty years' hard time.

Orrik endured several difficult years locked away in military prisons. Eventually he escaped to survive on the run for several months before one of his associates betrayed him to the authorities. His subsequent imprisonment was far harsher than the first, and there was even talk of sending him to Bloodshore Island. Orrik believed he was doomed to languish forgotten in confinement for the rest of his life.

The death of Vinter III and subsequent crowning of King Vinter IV bought Orrik a reprieve. No one was more surprised than he when the new king not only remembered him but also ordered his release. Saxon could no longer serve openly in the military, but Vinter IV made the former scout an agent of the Inquisition.

Saxon's gratitude cemented a loyalty to his master that outlasted the Lion's Coup. Without the intervention of Vinter IV, he would have been sent to Bloodshore Island to die in prison, and he has never forgotten that. He was among the inquisitors who sought to free Vinter IV from his imprisonment while he awaited trial and execution following the coup. Vinter solved that problem himself by making his now-famous escape. Word quickly reached Orrik that Vinter had drifted east on an airship across the impassable Bloodstone Marches.

For several long years Orrik survived on the fringes of civilization, keeping his identity a secret until he received a coded message confirming that Vinter had conquered a previously unknown species across the desert. Vinter's instructions to Orrik were simple: after passing along a separate packet of coded instructions to Head Inquisitor Dexer Sirac, Orrik was ordered to rejoin his liege in the east.

Vinter IV is famous for surviving his crossing, but Saxon Orrik repeated that feat without an airship to expedite his passage. He learned to hunt whatever slithering beasts he could for scraps of meat while finding inventive methods to procure water and shelter. By the time he rejoined his king, Orrik had become a master of the Bloodstone Desert. His crossing had forged him into the perfect man to guide the skorne back west.

Saxon Orrik has since forgotten any life but the sun, wind, and sands. The Bloodstone Desert is his home, and he has mastered its vastness. He trained the skorne to cross the desert and conduct their war. He has led the way countless times and seems to draw strength from the hellish clime. Saxon has established contacts among diverse groups willing to hire him for his lore of Immorese terrain. His reputation now stands quite separate from that of his master. Indeed, many of those who use his services neither know of nor care about his true loyalties. His dark eyes reveal less than his few words. Saxon Orrik's step unerringly guides those who follow his trail to their destination.

VIKTOR PENDRAKE
CYGNAR ALLY MINION CHARACTER SOLO

This land is blessed with an innumerable variety of species and variations of life. Morrow willing, I will document them all.

—Viktor Pendrake

PENDRAKE						
SPD	STR	MAT	RAT	DEF	ARM	CMD
6	6	6	6	14	14	9

CHAIN BOLA			
RNG	ROF	AOE	POW
8	1	—	—

LUCKY BOW			
RNG	ROF	AOE	POW
12	1	—	10

ORGOTH SWORD	
POW	P+S
5	11

DAMAGE	5
FIELD ALLOWANCE	C
POINT COST	2
SMALL BASE	

Minion – This model will work for Circle and Trollbloods.

Animosity [Saxon Orrik] – This model cannot be included in an army that includes one or more models of the listed type.

PENDRAKE

✠ **Fearless**

☾ **Pathfinder**

✪ **Tough**

Beast Lore (★Action) – RNG 3. Target friendly warrior model/unit. If the model/unit is in range, it gains boosted attack rolls against warbeasts for one turn.

Dismember – When this model hits a warbeast with a melee attack, roll an additional damage die.

Duck – This model gains +4 DEF against melee and ranged attack rolls made by warbeasts. Warbeasts cannot target this model with free strikes.

CHAIN BOLA

Cumbersome – If this model attacks with this weapon during its activation, it cannot attack with another ranged weapon that activation. If this model attacked with another ranged weapon this activation, it cannot attack with this weapon.

Knockdown – When a model is hit by an attack with this weapon, it is knocked down.

LUCKY BOW

Luck – This model can reroll missed attack rolls with this weapon. Each attack roll can be rerolled only once as a result of Luck.

ORGOTH SWORD

✪ **Magical Weapon**

A legend in his own time, Professor Viktor Pendrake has gained recognition across the Iron Kingdoms for adventurous daring and scholarly acumen. He has passed down wisdom gained from years spent in the wild by chairing the Department of Extraordinary Zoology at Corvis University. His research demands he place himself in peril in order to directly observe and interact with his subjects.

Pendrake's background as a Cygnaran army scout makes him uniquely suited to his current endeavors. Trained by the notorious Saxon Orrik, a young Pendrake witnessed atrocities committed by his mentor and felt compelled to report them. Rewarded for both his adherence to Cygnar's laws and his obvious skill as a ranger, Pendrake

TACTICAL TIPS

Chain Bola – This weapon does not cause damage.

rose through the ranks. Patrolling the borders for enemy insurgents proved to be not to his liking, but despite his reservations Pendrake became an exceptional officer. His first taste of real command came when his superiors entrusted him to lead an entire company of rangers before his twentieth summer.

After a risky reconnaissance run well past the Khadoran border, Pendrake's company was ambushed and slaughtered nearly to the last. After emerging as the sole survivor, Pendrake undertook desperate measures to retain the vital intelligence his company had gathered. In a now-famous incident, the young officer sought refuge amid a tribe of pygmy trolls, going so far as to strip down and disguise himself in mud and leaves in order to pass as one of them. This crazy ruse not only worked but also sparked within Pendrake a deeper love of studying wilderness creatures.

When he returned to civilization, Pendrake gave up military life to accept a post at Corvis University, where he began his career as an adventuring scholar and made his true name. He spent decades venturing into the wilds to study every monstrous creature he could find. During his travels he has had countless close brushes with death, many of which he recorded in his multivolume *Monsternomicon*.

After 603 AR Pendrake witnessed firsthand the skorne invasion and occupation of Corvis. His unique skills allowed him to become one of the few scholars to study this previously unknown species from across the Bloodstone Desert. Pendrake could see the future threat they might represent to Cygnar and felt duty-bound to offer his services to the Cygnaran Army as an expert in both the skorne and the Bloodstone Marches.

While investigating skorne attacks on friendly trollkin kriels, Pendrake walked into an ambush. His friend Quimut nearly died in this battle, and Pendrake himself was taken alive. He was hauled by titans back to the Abyssal Fortress in a cage. There he learned that Vinter Raelthorne and Saxon Orrik intended to lead a massive and well-equipped skorne army west. Pendrake's ordeal was not over: Vinter decided to send him east to document the greatness of the Skorne Empire, using propaganda written to undermine Cygnar's will to oppose him.

After a lengthy ordeal, Pendrake managed to escape and return west with new insight into the skorne threat. His unique knowledge and sense of duty drove him to put aside his scholarly pursuits, and he now uses his unmatched scope of lore and the friendships he has made abroad to assist the Cygnaran Army. He can go where the military cannot. With Khador knocking on Corvis' northern gate and skorne on the eastern front, Pendrake is glad to loan his sword to the fight, but those who know him understand that his most dangerous weapon is his mind.

Guilt hounds my every waking moment. I will drown that guilt in the blood of our enemies.

—Lanyssa Ryssyl

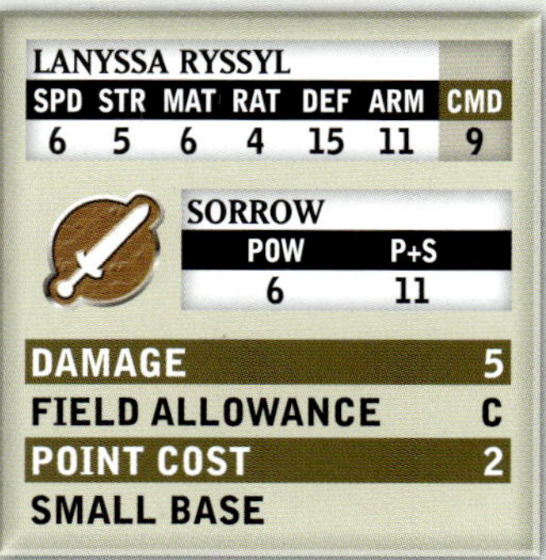

LANYSSA RYSSYL						
SPD	STR	MAT	RAT	DEF	ARM	CMD
6	5	6	4	15	11	9

SORROW		
	POW	P+S
	6	11

DAMAGE	5
FIELD ALLOWANCE	C
POINT COST	2
SMALL BASE	

Mercenary – This model will work for Cygnar and the Retribution.

Minion – This model will work for Circle and the Trollbloods.

Animosity [Legion or Blighted] – This model cannot be included in an army that includes one or more models of the listed type.

LANYSSA RYSSYL
Pathfinder

Magic Ability [7]

- **Hunter's Mark (★Attack)** – Hunter's Mark is a RNG 10 magic attack that causes no damage. Friendly models can charge or make a slam power attack against an enemy model hit by Hunter's Mark without being forced or spending focus. A friendly model charging an enemy model hit by Hunter's Mark gains +2˝ of movement. Hunter's Mark lasts for one turn.

- **Ice Bolt (★Attack)** – Ice Bolt is a RNG 10 magic attack. A model hit suffers a POW 12 cold damage roll. On a critical hit, the model hit becomes stationary for one round unless it has Immunity: Cold.

- **Winter Storm (★Action)** – Enemy models that begin their activation in this model's command range lose Eyeless Sight, Flight, and Pathfinder during their activations. Winter Storm lasts for one round.

Prowl – This model gains Stealth while within terrain that provides concealment, the AOE of a spell that provides concealment, or the AOE of a cloud effect.

Vendetta [Legion or Blighted] – This model gains boosted attack and damage rolls against Legion or Blighted models.

SORROW
Magical Weapon

Critical Freeze – On a critical hit, the model hit becomes stationary for one round unless it has Immunity: Cold.

TACTICAL TIPS

Magic Ability – Performing a Magic Ability special action or special attack counts as casting a spell.

Hunter's Mark – Modifiers to movement apply only to a model's normal movement.

By the standards of her long-lived race, Lanyssa Ryssyl is just entering the prime of life, but her experiences abroad have given her rare insight into the world beyond the Shard Spires. Though she did not stay to complete the formalities of her training, Ryssyl is a sorceress of considerable skill.

She might have spent a contented lifetime away from her homeland had she not received word of northern terrors and the cataclysm that nearly destroyed her people. Anger fills her over the devastation Everblight wrought, and she cannot ignore the guilt she feels over her absence during this crisis. In her calmer moments, however, she realizes she would not be the weapon she is now had she not tested her mettle in the far corners of Cygnar, Ord, Llael, and Khador.

Lanyssa arrived too late to participate in the last stand of the Nyss, finding only burned outposts and slaughter. This spark ignited the conflagration of her wrath, and she could not be kept from hunting down the nearest tendril of Legion forces. What followed was a hopeless battle near the Nyschatha Mountains. Though her friends fought bravely beside her, they inevitably fell one by one.

Journeying south to find other allies, Lanyssa became acquainted with the refugees of her people in Khador and made contact with both Cylena Raefyll and the Iosan mage hunter Eiryss. Lanyssa was among the first to learn of the fate of Nyssor and the unholy forces conspiring against the ailing god. Knowing Khadoran wizards stole the sacred vault of Nyssor, Lanyssa now devotes herself entirely to war against both the Legion of Everblight and the Khadoran Greylords.

Lanyssa Ryssyl has seen her people destroyed and their lands despoiled. She has seen despair in the faces of those few who survived, knowing all they once had is lost. Lanyssa has faced the horror that is the Legion of Everblight, and she has vowed to spend all her power as a sorceress to annihilate them.

She was not always like this. She earned her fame as one of the few Nyss to venture into warmer climes in search of adventure; in fact, Lanyssa was the first Nyss many inhabitants of the towns she visited had ever seen. Her cool beauty and sharp eyes intimidated many—as did the claymore slung across her feathered cloak. She eventually found friendship among a chosen few outside her species.

TOTEM HUNTER
MINION CHARACTER SOLO

The totem hunter stalks the land hunting man and beast as if they were one and the same.

—Professor Viktor Pendrake

TOTEM HUNTER						
SPD	STR	MAT	RAT	DEF	ARM	CMD
7	8	8	4	14	15	9

KELKAX

POW	P+S
6	14

SPIKED BUCKLER

POW	P+S
3	11

DAMAGE	8
FIELD ALLOWANCE	C
POINT COST	3
MEDIUM BASE	

Minion – This model will work for Circle, Legion, Skorne, and Trollbloods.

TOTEM HUNTER

✷ **Fearless**

☾ **Pathfinder**

⚑ **Stealth**

Hunter – This model ignores forests, concealment, and cover when determining LOS or making a ranged attack.

Jump – After using its normal movement to make a full advance but before performing an action, you can place this model anywhere completely within 5″ of its current location. Any effects that prevent it from charging also prevent it from using Jump.

Prey – After deployment but before the first player's turn, choose an enemy model/unit to be this model/unit's prey. This model gains +2 to attack and damage rolls against its prey. When this model begins its activation within 10″ of its prey, it gains +2″ movement that activation. When the prey is destroyed or removed from play, choose another model/unit to be the prey.

Sprint – At the end of this model's activation, if it destroyed one or more enemy models with melee attacks this activation it can make a full advance.

KELKAX

⊘ **Reach**

Immoren is but one of Caen's continents. The world is largely unexplored by its isolated inhabitants and contains horrors many of its denizens can barely fathom. Originating across the ocean, one of these frightening species is represented by a being known as the totem hunter. Very little is known about this creature's culture, beliefs, or native language, but its motive is clear: it lives to hunt. The totem hunter values its kills above all else and retains grisly totems from its most formidable adversaries. Its hunts are accompanied by sacred rituals through which the hunter hopes to capture a portion of each kill's essence.

Strengthened by its totemic trophies, the hunter seeks increasingly refined levels of lethal perfection. It is rarely seen by its victims except in the moment before death. With a hideous cry that can shatter glass and paralyze men in terror, it leaps from nowhere to impale its chosen target upon a wickedly barbed spear. This hunter has been drawn to the battles of western Immoren like a carrion crow to a charnel feast. Able to cloak itself in shadow and vanish into the darkness, the totem hunter leaves no trace of its passage other than whatever remains of its hapless targets.

TACTICAL TIPS

PREY – Modifiers to movement apply only to a model's normal movement.

This is a fortuitous time to seek trophies, for the rise of Everblight and the invasion of the skorne have brought more powerful and singular prizes for the totem hunter to harvest. Its complete lack of any other agenda means it is willing to join battle on any side: those who profit from its presence in one engagement might well find themselves at its mercy in the next.

The totem hunter makes itself known to a chosen battlefield commander shortly before an engagement, choosing those it considers worthy by its own inscrutable criteria. After drawing the eye of a warlock, it makes an enigmatic gesture—perhaps some form of salute—and vanishes. This motion indicates the totem hunter will spare the soldiers of its chosen leader. In the ensuing fight it preys upon any of the enemy's dangerous beasts or formidable combatants that draw its attention. It slips away after the battle without seeking any payment or recompense beyond the totems it gathered in the course of its bloody work.

The totem hunter has honed its skills with obsessive determination and bears many weapons of power. It can leap tremendous distances and meld seamlessly into cover. Indeed, any attempt to track the totem hunter after battle or engage in more extensive interaction ends with inevitable failure. Whatever its purpose in Immoren, there are few creatures as graceful, deadly, or utterly terrifying.

GATORMEN of WESTERN IMMOREN

BY TOOTH, CLAW, AND SPIRIT

The dark swamps and bayous of western Immoren harbor many dangers within their murky waters, and countless of those who dare travel their muddy byways meet a bad end in the gullet of some monstrous, amphibious beast. One race of elusive reptilians has claimed these bogs and marshes as their domain, furiously defending their way of life from the encroaching threat of civilization. The gatormen are incredibly tough, physically powerful, and skillful hunters that have long endured the challenges and dangers of their swamps. Though their appearance might lead some to believe them little more than savage beasts, gatormen possess a craftiness and intelligence that is the match of many more civilized species and display a high level of patience and cunning that makes them exceedingly dangerous predators.

Gatormen can be violent and even bloodthirsty at times, but if approached by outsiders with the proper respect and deference, they are often quite willing to trade for goods normally unavailable to them, and some may even be willing to act as guides. In fact, some gatormen have established peaceful relations with neighboring trollkin kriels and human settlements. Conversely, riled gatormen are some of the most implacable foes in western Immoren, especially in their natural habitat. Those who have earned the wrath of a gatorman tribe live with the fear that every floating log and tangled grove of cypress trees could hide a war party patiently waiting for their target to lower his guard.

Most gatormen live in small tribes numbering between a handful to several dozen adults. All adults are capable warriors, and there is little difference between the males and females in regard to size and physical prowess. Each tribe is led by one of its bokors, who are a combination of priest and mystic. These shamans invoke the name of Kossk, the bestial alligator god the gatormen worship, as well as calling forth the many lingering dark spirits that populate the bogs and marshes.

As often as not, the spirits bokors draw upon for their power are ones they enslaved at the time of death or caught in the aftermath of battles before they could pass on to Urcaen. Bokors rely on their own rites and totems to facilitate this, making use of skulls or other ritual tools carved of bone. Other long-dead allies under their control are the ancient and potent natural spirits that have existed within the swamp for millennia. The gatormen revere their greatest ancestors, and sometimes these spirits refuse to depart and instead haunt their ancestral lands, remaining violently territorial. The stagnant nature of the swamp

WORSHIP OF KOSSK

Gatormen across western Immoren pay homage to a primal alligator god they call Kossk, an entity they credit with their creation and which embodies feasting, reptilian patience, blood thirst, and the hunt. Though worship of this god is nearly universal among the gatormen, specific rites vary across the region, as do totemic depictions of it. In some areas it is shown as a gatorman, but in others it appears as a more bestial alligator, its gigantic maw open wide to swallow the world.

The leaders of religious ceremonies in their villages, bokors conduct sacrificial feasts and rites, calling on Kossk's name while invoking their magic. Each bokor has a different attitude toward this entity and the power it offers, with some relying more heavily upon minor spirits sought out and bound amid the swamps and marshes. Some bokors treat Kossk as simply the most powerful and greatest of these spirits rather than offering it the respect due a god.

Gatorman shamans draw upon the power of predatory spirits in the swamp as well. Just as Kossk prepares to devour the world and absorb its strength, the gatorman bokors and warlocks embrace the act of absorbing an enemy's power through the ritual consumption of its flesh. In fact, much of the dark magic and ritual that make up gatorman mysticism revolves around this concept.

Outsiders such as the blackclads of the Circle Orboros insist Kossk is a primitive totem embodying a single form of the Beast of All Shapes. It has been common throughout tribal cultures of various species for predatory totems to be identified and revered, each being a form of the Devourer Wurm, who encompasses them all. Gatorman bokors consider it blasphemous and disrespectful to link their faith to any other power and have reacted violently to blackclad efforts to take advantage of this alleged connection.

preserves these spirits and those of certain great reptilian beasts and allows them to grow over the centuries by feasting on the spiritual essences of other creatures that die within the fetid waters. Bokors can awaken these spirits by ritually feeding them with sacrifices of blood and life force, empowering them to lend their strength and vitality to the bokor and his allies or to inflict horrific curses on his enemies.

Despite being incredibly powerful warriors, the gatormen have largely remained uninvolved in the countless wars that have consumed western Immoren. Instead, they have focused their efforts on battling the other creatures dwelling in the dank swamps they inhabit. Their primary foe has been the bog trogs, fishlike humanoids skilled in ambushes and stealthy assassination. The two races have fought over the meager resources of western Immoren's swamps for longer than either can remember. However, the gatormen often have an advantage over the bog trogs, who lack powerful leadership and are individually weaker. In addition, the rare presence of gatorman warlocks, who command terrifying reptilian warbeasts, has further cemented their race's dominance in their natural habitat. Typically the bog trog tribes are either subjugated by their more powerful neighbors or driven out.

GATORMAN ORGANIZATION

Gatorman tribes are traditionally independent of one another and seldom cooperate. Indeed, fierce competition between rival tribes invariably leads to bloodshed when food supplies are scarce. Generally, each village is led by the most feared bokor. However, extraordinarily powerful bokors occasionally rise to bring multiple tribes together under their yoke, creating small fiefdoms within the deepest swamps and marshes.

Gatorman warriors are some of the most physically imposing combatants in all of Immoren. The typical gatorman stands well over seven feet tall and is armored head to tail in thick, horny scales. Though their natural armaments—tooth, claw, and whipping tail—are fearsome enough, gatorman warriors also wield a variety of heavy, two-handed crushing and cleaving weapons. So armed, gatorman hunting parties can reduce warjacks to scrap metal in minutes and a lone warrior can take on entire troops of enemies.

Gatormen are fiercely protective of their kills. In fact, it is the height of disrespect to consume the flesh of an enemy slain by another. To do so is to invite instant and lethal retaliation—or at the very least a lasting blood feud with the wronged gatorman.

Though gatorman warriors invariably make up the heart of any bokor's warband, other races, such as bog trogs, are often pressed into service. The bog trogs are simply given the option of adding their strength to that of the gatormen or else nourishing it with their flesh. Despite their strained relationship, bog trogs and gatormen complement each other's individual skills. Bog trogs bring numbers and an element of stealth and subtlety to gatorman warbands that is often lacking, and in turn, gatormen back up the bog trogs with their raw physical strength and toughness.

Another race found fighting alongside gatormen are the swamp gobbers. These creatures are hardly seen as a threat by gatormen and do not share the bog trogs' intensely adversarial relationship with them. In fact, swamp gobbers willingly work for gatorman bokors and warlocks in return for food and protection.

Stranger creatures, such as magic-eating horrors known as thrullgs and the incorporeal feralgeists, are captured or enslaved by the bokors and thrust into battle when their abilities are deemed useful. In addition, a number of the exotic froglike croaks that hail from the swamps and jungles of the distant east have recently sought protection from and offered their services to several influential bokors in the southern swamps. These creatures originated on islands to the south of territory held by the skorne, who captured them and hauled them into the west. The ones that have escaped find themselves far from home and seem to view the gatormen with superstitious reverence.

The gatormen are certainly powerful in their own right, but what makes them truly frightening is their command over the great and terrible beasts lurking within the murky depths of their swamps. Gatorman warlocks can call upon a number of horrific reptilian warbeast every bit as devastating on the battlefield as any found in western Immoren's various diverse fighting forces. The gatormen have an affinity with these monsters, and their own reptilian brains can slice through the bestial instincts that fill the mind of something like a bull snapper and command its actions. Gatorman bokors believe this ability is a gift from Kossk itself, allowing its children to command the creatures that bear its likeness.

Though gatormen are largely reclusive, they are sometimes willing to lend their strength to outsiders for suitable compensation. Many bokors have become shrewd negotiators capable of turning nearly any situation to their advantage. Gatormen will usually accept payment in food or metal weapons, which they typically do not produce on their own. Other demands often include the right to pick clean the battlefield, laying claim to both the enemy dead and all they carried. Gatormen value such personal possessions, whether given as a gift or seized in battle, believing each imparts some of its previous owner's vitality or cunning to the recipient.

Despite the contact with outside civilizations it brings, this mercenary activity has prompted little change in gatorman culture. Those who spend time fighting outside their swamps often bring back treasures and curiosities from their travels, but the gatormen rarely attempt to adopt the engineering advances of other cultures. Gatormen remain the same tribal people they have been for millennia.

THE BLINDWATER CONGREGATION

The swamp is a stagnant place where change comes slowly if at all. Like their waterlogged homelands, for many millennia the gatormen of western Immoren have resisted any major upheavals in their way of life. Now, however, the actions of an ambitious few threaten to alter the course of their history irreversibly. A powerful gatorman warlock and bokor known as Bloody Barnabas has united a number of large tribes around Blindwater Lake and Bloodsmeath Marsh. Barnabas is a truly ancient gatorman who has been stalking the swamps and devouring his foes for centuries. Over time he has conquered many gatorman tribes, both near Blindwater and beyond, to add their strength to his growing host of warriors, uniting them in a perpetual cycle of carnage and death.

Barnabas aspires to nothing short of godhood—to become a blood-drenched, gape-mawed, immortal horror even mightier than Kossk. To accomplish this, he seeks to gather a massive army of gatormen, bog trogs, and other swamp creatures beneath his banner and demonstrate his greatness to an extent that will compel their worship. He intends to lead his army in conquest after conquest until, soaked in the gore of thousands, he will push his followers into one final, grand confrontation. It is his hope that when he finally falls in battle, the dark energy of the countless deaths inflicted in his name coupled with the adoration of his living servants will trigger an apotheosis that will enable him to transcend his own death and join the ranks of the gods.

Barnabas is a feared and respected leader, but his grand designs require an attention to detail for which he has little patience. This has created an opportunity for other powerful gatorman warlocks, such as Calaban the Grave Walker, to take over those tasks in which he himself has no interest. An incredibly potent gatorman bokor, Calaban is cold, calculating,

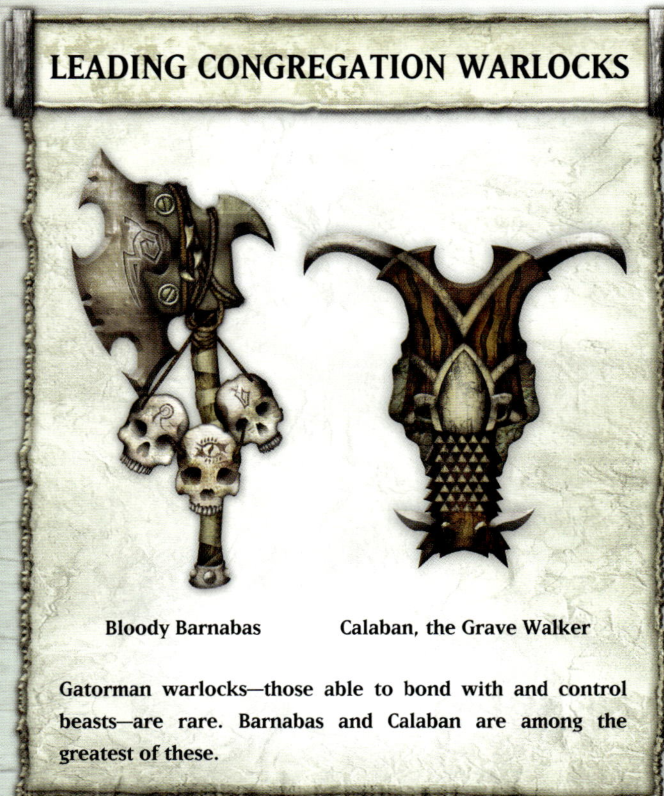

Bloody Barnabas   Calaban, the Grave Walker

Gatorman warlocks—those able to bond with and control beasts—are rare. Barnabas and Calaban are among the greatest of these.

and pragmatic where Barnabas is ruthlessly, even recklessly, ambitious. His knowledge of gatorman magic and ritual is unequaled, and he can call forth ancient and powerful spirits to do his bidding and lend strength to his various causes. Though he willingly aids Barnabas in his mad goals, Calaban is no fool; he has no intention of letting his own life force fuel the warlord's ambitions. Instead, he acts as the guiding hand behind Barnabas' conquests and campaign of domination, subtly turning the war host to his own ends.

Despite Calaban's vast mystical lore and access to powerful spiritual allies, his own goals are more earthbound. An exceedingly intelligent and progressive gatorman, he wishes to see his people grow beyond a collection of small tribes scattered across the swamps and marshes of western Immoren. He sees the work started by Barnabas in the Blindwater as the first step toward a larger unification of gatormen. Calaban envisions a day when the swamps belong to his people and his people alone, and all who enter their murky depths must pay tribute or feed the gatormen with their flesh. Barnabas is an integral part of Calaban's plans. He will use the ancient warrior and his legend to bring the gatormen together, and when Barnabas finally expires in a blaze of carnage, Calaban will find another to take his place at the fore of his growing gatorman army.

The Bloodsmeath boasts a large population of bog trogs, which have long battled the gatormen for control of the swamp. With Barnabas' unification of many of the larger gatorman tribes, the tide of this age-old battle quickly turned and Barnabas completely eradicated the dominant bog trog tribe in the Bloodsmeath. Before Barnabas could complete his wholesale slaughter of the Thornwood trogs, however, Calaban intervened and proposed a better solution: spare the bog trogs in exchange for their service to the Congregation. With little choice, the bog trogs agreed, and Calaban has made heavy use of their stealth and ambush tactics in further conquests both in the Bloodsmeath and beyond. At Calaban's direction Barnabas has collected gatorman warriors from the Marchfells and the Fenn Marsh, and he intends to continue to spread the word of his deeds to the farthest corners of the continent.

To have two of the most powerful warlocks of the species working together is a potent boon to the Congregation. Not only does their magical skill provide tremendous aid to the gatorman host, their ability to call forth mighty reptilian warbeasts from the depths of the swamp lends great might to the Blindwater Congregation. The monstrosities that serve Barnabas and Calaban are drawn from the remote depths of various swamps and bogs, and many have never been seen outside the myths and legends of those few humans that call these regions home.

Though often employed by the powers fighting on the fringes of western Immoren, the gatormen of Blindwater have taken little away from these associations beyond one thing: they have awoken to the allure of ambition and conquest. If Bloody Barnabas and Calaban have their way, the swamps of western Immoren will soon vomit forth a tide of blood and death, and those that once used the gatormen to fight their battles will fall beneath the snapping jaws and scaly tread of a terrifying gatorman horde.

CALABAN'S CADRE
THE SNAPPING JAWS OF THE GRAVE WALKER

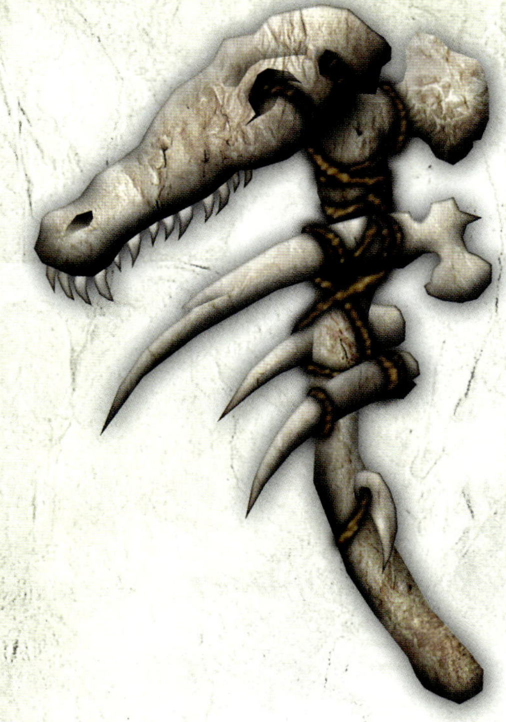

LEADERSHIP
Calaban, the Grave Walker
Bokor Agrek, Harkath, Nygor, and Varag

ASSETS
30 Bog trog ambushers
4 Croak hunters
12 Feralgeists
50 Gatorman posse warriors
4 Blackhide wrastlers
6 Bull snappers
3 Ironhide spitters

Calaban, the Grave Walker, is the organizing power behind the mad ascension of Bloody Barnabas, and it is largely left to the powerful gatorman warlock to command the great host of swamp creatures that constitute the Blindwater Congregation. However, Calaban never travels anywhere without a handpicked group of gatorman bokors and warriors as well as his favored warbeasts brought with him from the Fenn Marsh.

Unlike many bokors, Calaban does not always favor a direct and ferocious assault upon his enemies. When he and his personal warband enter battle he prefers subterfuge and misdirection to bring down his foes. Such tactics have allowed him to defeat far more powerful adversaries than normally possible for a warband of the size he commands.

Calaban and his cadre have single-handedly scored a number of decisive victories for the gatormen and have gone a long way in spreading the mysterious and deadly reputation of the Blindwater Congregation, particularly into the southern swamps. Most recently, they intercepted a large group of trollkin traveling toward the Thornwood through the Bloodsmeath Marsh. A pair of dire trolls and a number of full-blood trolls supported the trollkin, and the trollblood forces outnumbered Calaban and his warband two-to-one. Calaban, showing true reptilian patience, simply waited for the trolls to enter an area of deep and stagnant water rich with the energies of death from the countless people who had drowned there.

As the trollkin struggled to negotiate the deep swamp, gatormen, bog trogs, and massive reptilian warbeasts suddenly rose up from the mire to surround them completely. Calaban invoked his will to call on the dark powers of the place, and what followed was unmitigated slaughter. The trollkin were torn to pieces by Calaban's warbeasts or assaulted by the unending wave of dark, death-fed magic he sent forth. This victory over the trollkin netted the gatormen an impressive array of metal weapons and armor and further cemented Calaban's reputation as a bokor of unequaled skill.

BLOODY BARNABAS
MINION GATORMAN WARLOCK

I saw him once and it made my blood run cold. There is something terrible and unnatural about him, a hunger that makes all men feel like prey.

—Alten Ashley

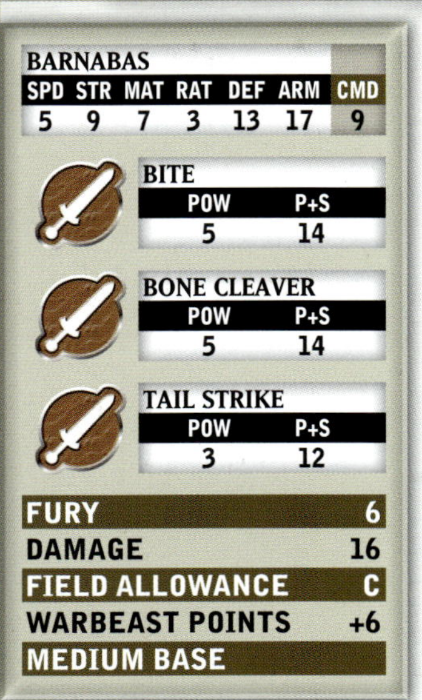

BARNABAS						
SPD	STR	MAT	RAT	DEF	ARM	CMD
5	9	7	3	13	17	9

BITE	
POW	P+S
5	14

BONE CLEAVER	
POW	P+S
5	14

TAIL STRIKE	
POW	P+S
3	12

FURY	6
DAMAGE	16
FIELD ALLOWANCE	C
WARBEAST POINTS	+6
MEDIUM BASE	

FEAT: BLACK TIDE

When Barnabas raises his axe and invokes a guttural call to the primal and savage powers worshipped by the gatormen, there arises a black flood of brackish waters that sweeps aside all who oppose him.

Non-amphibious enemy models currently in Barnabas' control area are knocked down.

Minion – This model will work for Circle, Legion, Skorne, and Trollbloods.

BARNABAS

⊛ Tough

Amphibious – This model ignores the effects of deep and shallow water and can move through them without penalty. While completely in deep water, it cannot be targeted by ranged or magic attacks and can make attacks only against other models in deep water. While completely in deep water, this model does not block LOS.

Counter Charge – When an enemy model advances and ends its movement within 6″ of this model and in its LOS, this model can immediately charge it. If it does, it cannot make another counter charge until after your next turn. This model cannot make a counter charge while engaged.

Gatorman Warlock – This model can have only Minion Gatorman warbeasts in its battlegroup.

Unyielding – While engaging an enemy model, this model gains +2 ARM.

BITE

Critical Consume – On a critical hit, if the attack hit a small-based non-warlock/warcaster model the model hit is removed from play.

BONE CLEAVER

⊘ Magical Weapon

⊘ Reach

Blood Boon – Once per activation, immediately after resolving an attack in which it destroyed a living enemy model with this weapon, this model can cast a spell with COST 3 or less without spending focus.

Gatormen do not die of old age, and rarely of illness. Their brutal lives almost invariably end in violence, when they are cut down by rivals or devoured by the monstrous predators infringing on their territory. The bokor known as Bloody Barnabas, however, stands as perhaps the oldest of his kind in all of western Immoren. Over time his name has come to mean not only death but absolute annihilation.

SPELLS	COST	RNG	AOE	POW	UP	OFF
FLESH EATER	3	10	–	13	NO	YES

When a living enemy model is boxed by Flesh Eater, it is removed from play and this model or a living warbeast in its battlegroup in its control area heals d3 damage points.

IRON FLESH	2	6	–	–	YES	NO

Target friendly warrior model/unit gains +3 DEF but suffers −1 SPD.

SWAMP PIT	2	CTRL	5	–	NO	NO

Place a 5″ AOE anywhere completely in this model's control area where it does not touch a model's base. The AOE is shallow water and remains in play for one round. While completely in a Swamp Pit AOE, a model with Amphibious cannot be targeted by ranged attacks.

WARPATH	2	SELF	CTRL	–	YES	NO

When a friendly Faction model in this model's control area destroys one or more enemy models with a melee or ranged attack during its activation, immediately after the attack is resolved, one warbeast in this model's battlegroup that is in its control area can advance up to 3″. A warbeast can advance only once per turn as a result of Warpath.

TACTICAL TIPS

Amphibious – This model can attack other models that are in deep water.

Flesh Eater – Because the boxed model is removed from play before being destroyed, it does not generate a soul or corpse token.

The gatormen do not venerate their elders; Barnabas has retained complete control over his tribe by his proven ruthlessness and apparent invincibility. The reverence and terror he inspires are as much due to the mad resolve seen in his unwavering stare as to his countless victories. He speaks with a measured calm and serene confidence born of a mind that knows no fear and is convinced of his superiority to everything that walks or breathes. Those who mistake his odd mannerisms for weakness or senility learn their mistake when he lashes out to destroy any he deems guilty of treachery; though he seems aloof, he notices all that transpires around him. He stands as the absolute tyrant of his people as well as a living terror to his enemies.

At the height of his earthly power, Barnabas has never been bested, but the years have begun to take a toll. He fears his body will soon fail, and this has forced him to turn his mind to larger aspirations. He intends to transcend his mortal shell as their new god, and nothing else matters to him. He believes his ascension requires becoming something greater than a legend in the minds of his people: they must leave behind their old beliefs and worship him. He will assemble all the gatormen under one banner to lead them into a great battle, and at the peak of slaughter and destruction, he will feast upon the energies of death. This energy combined with the reverence of his people will, so he believes, fuel his apotheosis.

Achieving this transformation will require considerable time, effort, and bloodshed, as there are many far-flung gatormen he must gather. Were his people less frightened of him they might question his wisdom in provoking terrible battles that cost so many lives. Yet with every passing year, more gatorman tribes and even outsiders learn of Bloody Barnabas, Terror of the Blindwater. His cult grows steadily, and with each new adherent he comes closer to his goal.

CALABAN, THE GRAVE WALKER
MINION GATORMAN WARLOCK

I know we will win. Our god is hungrier than theirs, as we are hungrier than they.

—Calaban, the Grave Walker

CALABAN						
SPD	STR	MAT	RAT	DEF	ARM	CMD
6	6	5	6	14	16	8

HEART STOPPER			
RNG	ROF	AOE	POW
10	2	—	10

BITE	
POW	P+S
5	11

CARCASS	
POW	P+S
5	11

FURY	7
DAMAGE	15
FIELD ALLOWANCE	C
WARBEAST POINTS	+6
MEDIUM BASE	

FEAT: DEATH HARVEST

Calaban revels in the fervor of slaughter and the feasting of his beasts and allies and can tap into the tremendous energies released by death. Amid the carnage he can freely call upon his magic and unleash an endless tide of destruction.

Each time a friendly model destroys an enemy model while the friendly model is in Calaban's control area, Calaban gains 1 fury point. Immediately after resolving an attack in which a model in Calaban's control area destroys one or more enemy models, Calaban can cast one spell. Calaban can boost attack and damage rolls on spells cast as a result of Death Harvest. Death Harvest lasts for one turn.

Minion – This model will work for Circle, Legion, Skorne, and Trollbloods.

CALABAN

Amphibious – This model ignores the effects of deep and shallow water and can move through them without penalty. While completely in deep water, it cannot be targeted by ranged or magic attacks and can make attacks only against other models in deep water. While completely in deep water, this model does not block LOS.

Gatorman Warlock – This model can have only Minion Gatorman warbeasts in its battlegroup.

HEART STOPPER

⊘ **Magical Weapon**

Grave Door – When a living enemy model is boxed by this attack, it heals 1 damage point. For the rest of the turn, this model can channel spells through the enemy model if it is in this model's control area and is not engaged. At the end of the turn, the enemy model is destroyed.

BITE

Sustained Attack – During this model's activation, when it makes an attack with this weapon against the last model hit by the weapon this activation, the attack automatically hits.

CARCASS

⊘ **Magical Weapon**

⊘ **Reach**

Life Trader – When an attack with this weapon hits, this model can suffer 1 damage point to gain an additional die on the damage roll against the model hit. Life Trader can be used once per attack.

SPELLS	COST	RNG	AOE	POW	UP	OFF
BONE SHAKER	2	8	–	12	NO	YES

When this spell boxes a living or undead non-warcaster, non-warlock enemy warrior model, you can immediately make a full advance with the enemy model followed by a normal melee attack, then the boxed model is removed from play. The boxed model cannot be targeted by free strikes during this movement.

CARNIVORE	2	6	–	–	YES	NO

Target friendly model/unit gains +2 to melee attack rolls against living models. When an affected model boxes a living model with a melee attack, the boxed model is removed from play and this model heals d3 damage points.

HEX BLAST	3	10	3	13	NO	YES

Enemy upkeep spells and animi on the model/unit directly hit by Hex Blast immediately expire.

OCCULTATION	2	6	–	–	YES	NO

Target friendly model/unit gains Stealth ⊘.

PARASITE	3	8	–	–	YES	YES

Target model/unit suffers –3 ARM and this model gains +1 ARM.

TACTICAL TIPS

DEATH HARVEST – Calaban still has to spend fury points to cast the spell.

AMPHIBIOUS – This model can attack other models that are in deep water.

BONE SHAKER – Because a boxed model is removed from play before being destroyed, it does not generate a soul or corpse token.

CARNIVORE – Because the boxed model is removed from play before being destroyed, it does not generate a soul or corpse token. This model, not the target model, is healed when the target model boxes another model.

HEX BLAST – Because they expire immediately, upkeep spells and animi that had an effect when the model/unit was hit or damaged will have no effect.

The bokor of the Fenn Marsh tribes speak of Calaban with fear and respect. No other of their number has so completely mastered the bloody rites by which they invoke the spirits of the dead as the calculating and shrewd Grave Walker. Having killed and devoured dozens of challengers, he is now one of the uncontested leaders of his people.

While other bokors of his power would command the loyalty of dozens of tribes, Calaban does not see himself as a chief or king. He prefers instead to be the voice of counsel to the greatest chieftains of his people and has linked his destiny to Bloody Barnabas of the Blindwater villages. He knows well the purpose behind Barnabas' plans but cares little. The ultimate unification of the tribes will be convenient for Calaban; in the short term Barnabas will either succeed and ascend or fail and be destroyed. In either event it will be Calaban who chooses the next figurehead and who will truly control the united gatormen. In the meantime the

escalating violence offers many opportunities for one who deals so intimately with death and the tormented spirits languishing in the fetid swamps of western Immoren.

Calaban revels in the opportunity to slaughter and steal spilled vitality for his own use. Wading into the bloodiest battles, he becomes an incarnation of gatorman appetites as he alternates killing and weaving vile curses and spells. Each battle is a welcome harvest of death for the Grave Walker.

BULL SNAPPER
MINION GATORMAN LIGHT WARBEAST

Careful. He's only asleep now because he's still digesting the last poor guy who didn't think he'd wake up.

—Alten Ashley

BULL SNAPPER						
SPD	STR	MAT	RAT	DEF	ARM	CMD
6	7	5	1	13	14	6

BITE		
	POW	P+S
H	5	12

FURY	3
THRESHOLD	7
FIELD ALLOWANCE	U
POINT COST	3
MEDIUM BASE	

BULL SNAPPER

Amphibious – This model ignores the effects of deep and shallow water and can move through them without penalty. While completely in deep water, it cannot be targeted by ranged or magic attacks and can make attacks only against other models in deep water. While completely in deep water, this model does not block LOS.

Blood Thirst – When it charges a living model, this model gains +2″ movement.

Man-Eater – This model can charge living warrior models without being forced.

Torpid – If this model destroys a living enemy model with a normal melee attack, this model's activation ends immediately after the attack is resolved and you can remove 1 fury point from this model.

BITE

Sustained Attack – During this model's activation, when it makes an attack with this weapon against the last model hit by the weapon this activation, the attack automatically hits.

ANIMUS	COST	RNG	AOE	POW	UP	OFF
SPINY GROWTH	2	6	–	–	NO	NO

Target friendly Faction model gains +2 ARM. If a warjack or warbeast hits the affected model with a melee attack, the attacking model suffers d3 damage points immediately after the attack has been resolved unless the affected model was destroyed or removed from play by the attack. Spiny Growth lasts for one round.

TACTICAL TIPS

AMPHIBIOUS – This model can attack other models that are in deep water.

BLOOD THIRST – Modifiers to movement apply only to a model's normal movement.

Though not as large as the blackhide wrastlers that terrorize the marshes of western Immoren, snappers have gained a fearsome reputation. Most outsiders see the creatures only in their resting state, as they lie in wait hoarding their energy amid the shallows or along the riverbanks. Left undisturbed, the snapper remains so still it seems dead, yet this belies a predatory watchfulness. Once roused by hunger or a perceived threat, they are capable of swift and deadly motion, going from a statutory stillness to lunging attack with no transition.

The males of the species, called bulls, have aggressive demeanors and enormous appetites and do not discriminate between prey. They are just as content to chew apart men or beasts as to gorge upon the giant catfish of the swamps that is their typical diet. Once a bull's jaws close upon its prey the reptile quickly tears it asunder and swallows in great gulps. Though temporarily sated, the bull is a voracious hunter and soon feels the urge to feast again. Anything disturbing a resting snapper soon feels the fury of its need to satisfy its bottomless appetite.

BLACKHIDE WRASTLER
MINION GATORMAN HEAVY WARBEAST

It may be a messy eater, but you have to admire its technique.
—Lynus Wesselbaum

ANIMUS	COST	RNG	AOE	POW	UP	OFF
RISE	1	6	–	–	NO	NO

Target friendly knocked down Faction model immediately stands up.

TACTICAL TIPS

RISE – This animus can affect a model that was knocked down this turn.

AMPHIBIOUS – This model can attack other models that are in deep water.

WRASTLER – Once knocked down, this model can remain knocked down and does not have to stand up. It can be in melee with enemy models while knocked down. While knocked down, this model's DEF is still reduced and it is automatically hit with melee attacks.

SNACKING – Because the boxed model is removed from play before being destroyed, it does not generate a soul or corpse token.

The black waters of the Bloodsmeath Marsh are still, like a darkened mirror. Only when the surface erupts into the gaping, black-scaled maw of a monstrous reptile does the true savagery of the swamp reveal itself. The creature surges upward to close its jaws around its prey and drag the hapless victim down to a churning death. Only a spreading crimson stain amid quiet ripples is left on the surface to mark the wake of the violence.

WRASTLER

Amphibious – This model ignores the effects of deep and shallow water and can move through them without penalty. While completely in deep water, it cannot be targeted by ranged or magic attacks and can make attacks only against other models in deep water. While completely in deep water, this model does not block LOS.

Man-Eater – This model can charge living warrior models without being forced.

Wrastler – While knocked down, this model can make attacks, has a melee range, can engage other models, can be engaged, and can use its animus.

Snacking – When this model boxes a living model with a melee attack, this model can heal d3 damage points. If this model heals, the boxed model is removed from play.

BITE

Death Roll (★Attack) – On a hit, before rolling damage you can decide to knock down both this model and the model it hit. If both models are knocked down, this damage roll is boosted.

CLAW
Open Fist

WRASTLER						
SPD	STR	MAT	RAT	DEF	ARM	CMD
5	12	6	1	12	19	6

BITE		
	POW	P+S
H	5	17

CLAW		
	POW	P+S
L	2	14

CLAW		
	POW	P+S
R	2	14

FURY	4
THRESHOLD	8
FIELD ALLOWANCE	U
POINT COST	9
LARGE BASE	

As the gatorman warlocks make their power known, the great blackhide wrastlers have become crucial to their schemes. The enormous gators possess a hunger awesome even by the standards of the voracious bokor beastmasters. Motivated by little more than the scent of blood or the promise of food, the huge beasts hurl themselves among enemies, biting even the largest in prey in two. Those they cannot readily eviscerate they drag into the water to be torn limb-from-limb as the wrastler contorts in a terrible feeding frenzy. Even as the wrastler consumes its gruesome feast, its own wounds close and its hunger begins to grow once more.

IRONBACK SPITTER
MINION GATORMAN HEAVY WARBEAST

It's ugly as sin with a temperament to match. If it doesn't snap you in half with its beak, it may just dissolve you into a formless slurry with its acidic vomit. Isn't nature grand?

—Alten Ashley

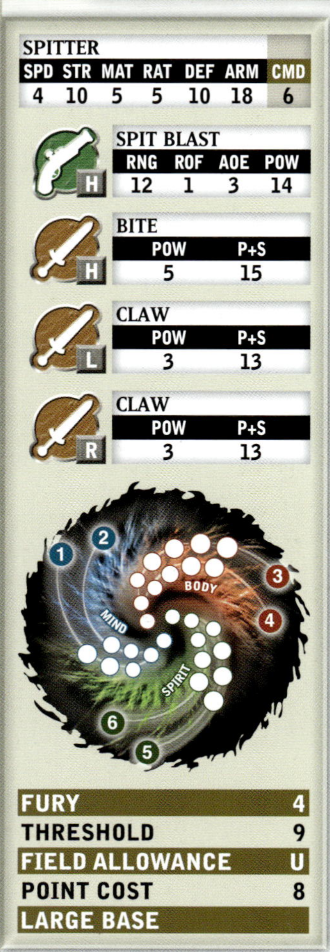

SPITTER						
SPD	STR	MAT	RAT	DEF	ARM	CMD
4	10	5	5	10	18	6

SPIT BLAST			
RNG	ROF	AOE	POW
12	1	3	14
H

BITE	
POW	P+S
5	15
H

CLAW	
POW	P+S
3	13
L

CLAW	
POW	P+S
3	13
R

FURY	4
THRESHOLD	9
FIELD ALLOWANCE	U
POINT COST	8
LARGE BASE	

SPITTER

Amphibious – This model ignores the effects of deep and shallow water and can move through them without penalty. While completely in deep water, it cannot be targeted by ranged or magic attacks and can make attacks only against other models in deep water. While completely in deep water, this model does not block LOS.

Back Plates – When a model hits this model with a free strike attack, immediately after the attack is resolved the attacking model suffers d6 damage points.

Girded – This model does not suffer blast damage. Friendly models B2B with it do not suffer blast damage.

SPIT BLAST

Continuous Effect: Corrosion

Damage Type: Corrosion

CLAWS

Open Fist

ANIMUS	COST	RNG	AOE	POW	UP	OFF
ORNERY	2	SELF	–	–	NO	NO

This model gains Retaliatory Strike. Ornery expires after the affected model makes a Retaliatory Strike attack. Ornery lasts for one round. (When a model with Retaliatory Strike is hit by a melee attack made by an enemy model during your opponent's turn, after the attack is resolved it can immediately make one normal melee attack against that enemy model.)

TACTICAL TIPS

AMPHIBIOUS – This model can attack other models that are in deep water.

Even gatormen are prey for ironbacks, but the most powerful bokors and warlocks among them have learned to tame the huge turtle-like creatures. A single spitter can be decisive on the battlefield, its vicious temper proving an asset as it spews hideous death at anything it encounters.

Of the creatures that dwell in the dank swamps of western Immoren, the ironback spitter is among the most feared. Despite its massive bulk, it can be hard to identify in its lurking places among the muck and wild vegetation. It is not uncommon for an unwary victim to tread directly upon its back before realizing the mistake. By that time, it is too late for caution: the notoriously ill-tempered chelonian rises to its full height as its claws reach out to rend its victim asunder.

These beasts are even more dangerous when actively hunting. Possessed of an indiscriminate appetite, the ironback will attack nearly anything to satisfy its hunger, though many seem to prefer small, bipedal creatures such as bog trogs or humans. Once it spies a suitable meal, it spits forth a great volume of noxious gastric acids accumulated in specialized bladders connected to its stomach. Anything unfortunate enough to be struck by this foul liquid is rendered into a pile of nutritious sludge.

Makes me smile to see a bunch of walkin' fish leap from the muck to pull their quarry down.
—Grim Angus

TACTICAL TIPS

AMPHIBIOUS – This model can attack other models that are in deep water.

CAMOUFLAGE – If a model ignores concealment or cover, it also ignores concealment or cover's Camouflage bonus.

The fiercely territorial and primitive amphibians known as bog trogs thrive in swampy regions considered undesirable by humans and other more civilized species. Conflicts with gatormen who inhabit similar regions are common, and in recent years several bog trog tribes have been coerced into assisting these erstwhile enemies in battles against outsiders. Bog trogs are peerless masters of ambush, swimming silently and unseen just below the surface of a stream, river, or shallow pond before springing to attack. In or out of the water they can change the color of their skin to blend effortlessly into their environment.

Minions – These models will work for Circle, Legion, Skorne, and Trollbloods.

LEADER & GRUNTS

 Combined Melee Attack

 Pathfinder

Ambush – You can choose not to deploy this unit at the start of the game. If it is not deployed normally, you can put it into play at the end of any of your Control Phases after your first turn. When you do, choose any table edge except the back of your opponent's deployment zone. Place all models in this unit in formation within 3″ of the chosen table edge.

Amphibious – This model ignores the effects of deep and shallow water and can move through them without penalty. While completely in deep water, it cannot be targeted by ranged or magic attacks and can make attacks only against other models in deep water. While completely in deep water, this model does not block LOS.

Camouflage – This model gains an additional +2 DEF when benefiting from concealment or cover.

FISH HOOK

 Reach

Powerful Charge – This model gains +2 to charge attack rolls with this weapon.

LEADER & GRUNTS						
SPD	STR	MAT	RAT	DEF	ARM	CMD
5	6	6	3	12	14	8

FISH HOOK		
	POW	P+S
	5	11

FIELD ALLOWANCE	2
LEADER & 5 GRUNTS	5
LEADER & 9 GRUNTS	8
SMALL BASE	

Whether manipulated, goaded, enslaved, or lured, large numbers of bog trogs have emerged to enter the recent struggles across the wilds of western Immoren. Such trogs have launched ruthless attacks from a variety of waterways, including the Fenn Marsh, the Bloodsmeath Marsh, the Marchfells, and the shores and rivers of Scarleforth Lake—all in the name of their allies and masters. Because few outsiders know the trogs' Quor-og tongue, communicating with them is difficult for most. Gatormen share a root language with the trogs, making them one of the few races with whom the trogs can regularly interact. Requiring little prompting to initiate ambushes, the trogs seem to take cruel delight in killing any creature caught in their path and plundering the bodies of the slain.

GATORMAN POSSE
MINION UNIT

They are creatures driven by simple hunger. The very smell of blood transforms them into paragons of slaughter.

—*Lord Tyrant Hexeris*

LEADER & GRUNTS						
SPD	STR	MAT	RAT	DEF	ARM	CMD
5	8	7	3	12	16	8

BITE

POW	P+S
5	13

GATORMAN WEAPON

POW	P+S
5	13

DAMAGE	8 EA
FIELD ALLOWANCE	2
LEADER & 2 GRUNTS	6
LEADER & 4 GRUNTS	9
MEDIUM BASE	

Minions – These models will work for Circle, Legion, Skorne, and Trollbloods.

LEADER & GRUNTS

✪ **Fearless**

Amphibious – This model ignores the effects of deep and shallow water and can move through them without penalty. While completely in deep water, it cannot be targeted by ranged or magic attacks and can make attacks only against other models in deep water. While completely in deep water, this model does not block LOS.

Blood Thirst – When it charges a living model, this model gains +2″ movement.

Prayers - The Leader of this unit can recite one of the following prayers each turn anytime during its unit's activation. Each model in this unit gains the benefits listed.

- **Cold Blood** - Affected models can reroll missed attack rolls against living models this turn. Each roll can be rerolled only once as a result of Cold Blood.

- **Dirge of Mists** – Affected models gain +1 DEF and Terror ✪ for one round.

- **March** – Affected models gain Pathfinder ◐ for one turn.

Unyielding – While engaging an enemy model, this model gains +2 ARM.

GATORMAN WEAPON

⊘ **Reach**

Though they are fierce combatants, when left to their own devices gatormen are generally content to guard their territories rather than seek excuses to fight. Few other species can communicate in the obscure Quor-gar dialect, but gatormen respond to gestures and simple commands. Their even-tempered dispositions outside of battle make them approachable by those seeking to barter for their services. Trollkin shamans and Circle Orboros druids alike have made such arrangements over the years, but the savage reptiles have no qualms about fighting for any species that offers them ample food.

Despite this reputation, in recent years several bloodthirsty and particularly formidable bokors have begun to stir gatorman villages to greater activity. These leaders are drawing together for mutual plunder and feasting. This rise in violent activity is an ominous sign of events to come for all who live on the fringes of the swamps and waterways.

Gatormen are among the most formidable warriors of all the savage species thriving in the wilderness of western Immoren. Few intelligent races can rival the raw killing power of these bipedal reptiles, which lurk in remote swamps and along riverbanks across the region. Gatormen are as adept striking with their heavy pole arms as they are with their natural weapons, such as their powerful flesh-rending jaws. A single gatorman can tear apart several well-armed men in a few short seconds, and the sight of blood drives them to a frenzy of carnage.

Their crude villages often include shrines in the shape of a tremendous alligator, icons to their bestial god Kossk. Leading gatorman shamans, or bokors, call upon their savage magic to drive bands of gatormen into bloodthirsty furor.

SWAMP GOBBER BELLOWS CREW
MINION UNIT

I don't care what that cloud smells like—it'll hide us from those archers, and we're going in.
—Greygore Boomhowler

TACTICAL TIPS

CAMOUFLAGE – If a model ignores concealment or cover, it also ignores concealment or cover's Camouflage bonus.

Swamp gobbers are a clever and hardy race of diminutive humanoids found in many bogs and marshes, but they are particularly numerous in the eastern Thornwood and the Widower's Wood outside Corvis. Their crowning achievement is a unique mixture of brewed liquids that combines with astonishing rapidity to produce a dense fog. They have been able to turn this innovation into an economic resource by inventing an ingenious contraption that spreads the fog across a large area, making it difficult to see anything more than a few feet away.

Half as tall as humans, gobbers possess chameleon-like skin that can change color to help them blend into their surroundings. Most gobbers are quite intelligent and have a natural knack for invention and alchemy, but some of the more isolated groups lack the sophistication of their more urbane peers. Swamp gobbers fall into this second category, though they do speak a variety of languages to barter trade for their villages.

Recent warfare has encouraged swamp gobbers to seek advantages for themselves. A number of these enterprising

Minions – These models will work for Circle, Legion, Skorne, and Trollbloods.

LEADER & GRUNT

Camouflage – This model gains an additional +2 DEF when benefiting from concealment or cover.

Cloud Cover (Order) – Models who received this order must forfeit their actions. After this unit's normal movement, place a 3″ AOE cloud effect in play with its center point within 1″ of the Leader. If the Grunt is B2B with the Leader, place a 5″ AOE instead. This AOE remains in play for one round.

LEADER & GRUNT						
SPD	STR	MAT	RAT	DEF	ARM	CMD
6	3	3	3	15	11	7

HAND WEAPON		
	POW	P+S
	2	5

FIELD ALLOWANCE	1
LEADER & 1 GRUNT	1
SMALL BASE	

folk have offered their services in return for food or weapons to be sent back to their families. Their prices are reasonable, and both the trollkin and druids have occasionally enlisted their particular expertise in concealment. This intrepid philosophy has put the swamp gobbers in harm's way like never before, and some of their tribes have been captured by the skorne or forced to serve the Legion. The bellows crew prefers not to fight if they can avoid it, their primary purpose instead being to use their fog to protect their allies against volleys of arrows, bullets, or skorne reiver needles.

CROAK HUNTER
MINION SOLO

—*Professor Viktor Pendrake*

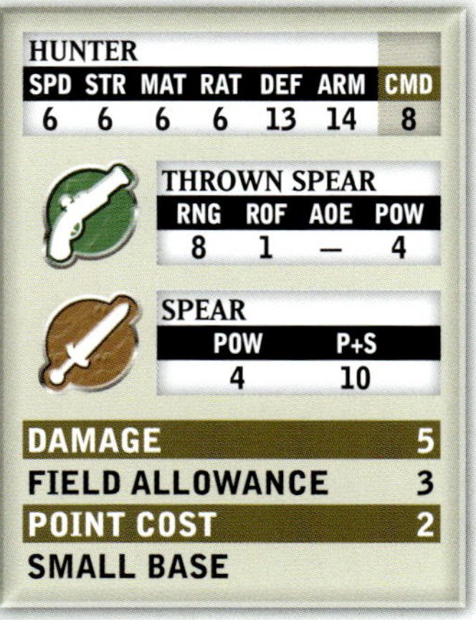

HUNTER						
SPD	STR	MAT	RAT	DEF	ARM	CMD
6	6	6	6	13	14	8

THROWN SPEAR			
RNG	ROF	AOE	POW
8	1	—	4

SPEAR	
POW	P+S
4	10

DAMAGE	5
FIELD ALLOWANCE	3
POINT COST	2
SMALL BASE	

Minion – This model will work for Circle, Legion, Skorne, and Trollbloods.

HUNTER

- Advance Deployment
- Immunity: Corrosion
- Pathfinder
- Stealth

Amphibious – This model ignores the effects of deep and shallow water and can move through them without penalty. While completely in deep water, it cannot be targeted by ranged or magic attacks and can make attacks only against other models in deep water. While completely in deep water, this model does not block LOS.

Gang Fighter – When making a melee attack targeting an enemy model in melee range of another friendly Faction warrior model, this model gains +2 to melee attack and melee damage rolls.

Hunter – This model ignores forests, concealment, and cover when determining LOS or making a ranged attack.

Vitriol – If this model is hit by a melee attack, immediately after the attack is resolved the attacking model suffers the Corrosion continuous effect unless this model was destroyed or removed from play by the attack.

THROWN SPEAR

Poison – Gain an additional die on this weapon's damage rolls against living models.

Thrown – Add this model's STR to the POW of this ranged attack.

SPEAR

- Reach

Poison – Gain an additional die on this weapon's damage rolls against living models.

TACTICAL TIPS

AMPHIBIOUS – This model can attack other models that are in deep water.

advantage of this credulity, and many croak hunters have allied with them. Some trollkin leaders have also gained the allegiance of the croak hunters, who find themselves drawn to swamp trolls as some sort of long-lost kin. Because the croak hunters are superb hunters and trackers, their services are much sought after.

Croak hunters coat their weaponry in poisons secreted from their own skin, an advantage that enables them to bring down larger prey than they would otherwise be able to. They strike at their prey from ambush, hurling poisoned spears before vanishing into the brush. Once confident of their imminent victory, croak hunters fill the air with warbled battle cries as they close on their victims.

Anura—or croaks, as most call them—are newcomers to western Immoren. This amphibious species originates from the Shattered Spine islands south of the Skorne Empire. Croak hunters are primitive but skilled members of a tribal culture well suited to survival in the hostile jungles of the archipelago. Several tribes enslaved by the skorne were brought west, and some escaped into the wilds. These adaptable creatures have made alliances with numerous individuals and groups.

Anxious to survive and ignorant of the natural order of their new home, the croak hunters hold some of the denizens of the region in religious awe. The gatormen of the Blindwater Congregation have been quick to take

There be a power in that eye o' his, gleamin' in the darkness and invokin' all manner o' vile slithery unpleasantness.
—Therin, elder of a swampy bayou village off the Black River

SPELLS	COST	RNG	AOE	POW	UP	OFF
INFLUENCE	1	10	–	–	NO	YES

Take control of target enemy non-warcaster, non-warlock warrior model. The model immediately makes one normal melee attack, then Influence expires.

| VOODOO DOLL | 2 | 8 | – | – | NO | YES |

Choose one of target enemy warbeast's aspects. That aspect suffers the effects of being lost for one round. A warbeast cannot be destroyed as a result of Voodoo Doll.

TACTICAL TIPS

AMPHIBIOUS – This model can attack other models that are in deep water.

LESSER WARLOCK – This model's type is solo, not warlock.

Some things lurk deep in the swamps and forgotten waterways, things man was not meant to know. Chief among them are the cunning gatormen, as hungry as their simpler relatives but smart enough to shape tools and weapons. Some possess a keen insight into the spirit world, the energies of blood and death, and the forces that lurk unseen in the fetid darkness. Gatormen base their faith on the central notion of predation and the cycle of hunger, hunting, and death. For one entity to be satiated it must consume another. This dark and foreboding belief fuels the power of a great bokor known as Wrong Eye. All who live in

Mercenaries – These models will work for Cryx.

Minions – These models will work for Circle, Legion, Skorne, and Trollbloods.

WRONG EYE

✠ **Fearless**

Amphibious – This model ignores the effects of deep and shallow water and can move through them without penalty. While completely in deep water, it cannot be targeted by ranged or magic attacks and can make attacks only against other models in deep water. While completely in deep water, this model does not block LOS.

Gatorman Warlock – This model can have only Minion Gatorman warbeasts in its battlegroup.

Lesser Warlock – This model is not a warlock but has the following warlock special rules: Battlegroup Commander, Control Area, Damage Transference, Forcing, Fury Manipulation, Healing, and Spellcaster.

BITE

Life Drinker – When it destroys a living enemy model with this weapon, immediately after the attack is resolved this model heals d3 damage points.

SWAMP HOOK

⊘ **Reach**

WRONG EYE						
SPD	STR	MAT	RAT	DEF	ARM	CMD
5	8	6	3	12	17	9

BITE		
	POW	P+S
	5	13

SWAMP HOOK		
	POW	P+S
	4	12

FURY	4
DAMAGE	8
FIELD ALLOWANCE	C
WRONG EYE & SNAPJAW	9
MEDIUM BASE	

the bayous of western Immoren know of his legend and hope to avoid his capricious wrath.

The mind of the gatorman is not like the mind of a man, a fact those who deal with the shaman would do well to remember. Wrong Eye emerges from the humid damp like a reptilian oracle. Those who look him in the eye immediately sense they face an entity of unfathomable thoughts. Any negotiation with Wrong Eye brings the possibility of bloodshed and feeding frenzy. Even hardened blackclads and trollkin champions sometimes lose their nerve and offer him more favorable terms than they might have initially intended.

Wrong Eye is an element of dangerous unpredictability akin to an alligator lying in a shallow river. When it rests unmoving like a log, it is impossible to tell whether such a creature has just eaten or waits ready to strike. Wrong Eye presents himself as amiable and polite in most cases, a sophisticated and keenly intelligent representative of his species. But tales persist of him suddenly erupting into murderous rage at the slightest perceived insult. Those who have dealt with him successfully insist the easiest way to maintain his more whimsical and friendly demeanor is to lavish him with small baubles.

The outward accoutrements with which the gatorman adorns himself are the best clues to the inner workings of his enigmatic mind. Those ignorant of his legend might find his appearance comical, but such an impression quickly fades. Wrong Eye is a fiercely curious and acquisitive being whose shamanism draws on the concept of consuming the power of others. All he kills becomes a part of his spiritual arsenal, and dark rumors insist he is a connoisseur of the flesh of other intelligent species. The creative impulse of mankind holds morbid fascination for Wrong Eye. He has adorned himself to imitate humanity for this reason, wearing attire either cobbled together in mimicry or stolen from those he has stalked and consumed.

Those few with the vision to see manifestations of the dead know many spirits linger near Wrong Eye, unable to leave his side even as they loathe him. The slightest hint of spiritual sensitivity enables one to hear their whispers, half-coherent warnings, or sudden sharp gasps of startled pain. Whether Wrong Eye even notices them is unclear: his stare is cold and impassive, and his toothy smile reveals nothing.

Wrong Eye shapes dolls he uses to influence others, driving needles through their limbs to make his chosen victims suffer by proxy. He wears a vest of bones and other tokens as elements of the elaborate spiritual armor warding him from danger. One could dismiss Wrong Eye's peculiar notions were it not for the actual power he demonstrates. With a single look from behind his oversized ocular, Wrong Eye compels weaker-willed creatures to caper and spasm.

ANIMUS	COST	RNG	AOE	POW	UP	OFF
SUBMERGE	2	SELF	–	–	NO	NO

This model cannot be targeted by ranged or magic attacks and does not block LOS. Submerge lasts for one round.

TACTICAL TIPS

Amphibious – This model can attack other models that are in deep water.

Blood Thirst – Modifiers to movement apply only to a model's normal movement.

Warbeast Bond [Wrong Eye] – Because the boxed model is removed from play before being destroyed, it does not generate a soul or corpse token.

When potential employers address him with the proper formality and respect, they find their courtesies returned. Wrong Eye sees himself as a shrewd manipulator of the factions employing him and deems no mortal his superior. His arrogance in this regard is certainly part of his madness, but the true power brokers seem to find him amusing and useful enough to overlook his eccentricities. Certainly his tremendous guardian has helped preserve him from easy retaliation.

Anyone dealing with Wrong Eye must also endure the lurking threat of the reptile Snapjaw. This oversized alligator prefers to linger near its master submerged below the calm surface of a shallow pool or gently flowing river. It can stay in this posture for hours, serene and unmoving like a dead thing, never so much as blinking or twitching its limbs. Yet the moment Wrong Eye compels it, the great beast leaps from the water with blinding speed to consume men whole or shatter boats to kindling with its heavily muscled tail.

The legends of Wrong Eye always depict Snapjaw standing ready to strike. Other bokors describe the creature in terms usually reserved for great spirits, not living beasts. They believe it to be a physical embodiment of Wrong Eye's inner nature, a manifestation of his great awakened power.

Though unimaginably fierce when goaded by his bokor, Snapjaw is otherwise a lazy hunter content to steal easy pickings. Wayward children wallowing in streams too far from home are a preferred snack. It is equally content to eat any livestock or unfortunate pets that happen to cross its path.

Wrong Eye sometimes lets Snapjaw wander off into settled regions to see what it can find. The bokor takes grim amusement in following at a distance and watching as the creature stirs up the small human communities. The gatorman chortles as locals try to rally and drive the beast away. Feeble efforts of local militia armed with pitchforks and other crude farm implements have never done more than scratch Snapjaw's scaled hide.

SNAPJAW

Amphibious – This model ignores the effects of deep and shallow water and can move through them without penalty. While completely in deep water, it cannot be targeted by ranged or magic attacks and can make attacks only against other models in deep water. While completely in deep water, this model does not block LOS.

Blood Thirst – When it charges a living model, this model gains +2″ movement.

Companion [Wrong Eye] – This model is included in any army that includes Wrong Eye. If Wrong Eye is destroyed or removed from play, remove this model from play. This model is part of Wrong Eye's battlegroup.

Man-Eater – This model can charge living warrior models without being forced.

Warbeast Bond [Wrong Eye] – Snapjaw is bonded to Wrong Eye. When Snapjaw boxes a living model with a melee attack in Wrong Eye's control area, the model is removed from play and either Snapjaw or Wrong Eye heals d3 damage points.

TAIL

⊘ Reach

Critical Knockdown – On a critical hit, the model hit is knocked down.

SNAPJAW						
SPD	STR	MAT	RAT	DEF	ARM	CMD
5	11	6	1	12	18	6

BITE (H)

POW	P+S
6	17

TAIL (–)

POW	P+S
3	14

FURY	4
THRESHOLD	8
FIELD ALLOWANCE	C
LARGE BASE	

Snapjaw's eyes never waver from its prey, and it closes with absolute conviction while ignoring any injuries. The only instinct it feels is ancient primordial hunger, and it will continue to devour until it drowns the ache in its belly in a tide of meat and blood. Wrong Eye likes to think he provides all the brains required for the pair, but given his dubious sanity that is little comfort to anyone confronted by them.

FARROW of WESTERN IMMOREN

CONQUEST BY BLOODY CLEAVER

Tribes of farrow have lived on the barren fringes of western Immoren for centuries. The species has often been overlooked by humanity except when farrow have led raids on remote townships or ambushes on trade caravans. They are a rugged and tribal people accustomed to doing what they must to survive. While their technologies are crude by human standards, farrow are an ingenious race that has proven remarkably adaptable.

In recent years farrow have offered services for hire in the escalating battles and wars among the greater powers around them. Mercenary labor has brought a wealth of battlefield experience and opportunities for scavenging and plunder. Whether they continue to be content fighting at the bidding of others or shape their own destiny will depend on the successes of their increasingly capable leaders.

FIGHTING FOR SCRAPS

The farrow have a reputation as scavengers, bandits, and ruthless opportunists, a reputation they both deserve and embrace. Farrow consider survival the foremost imperative and have no stigma against stealing anything not nailed down. The next highest priority in a farrow's life is to improve his standing compared to that of his peers, preferably dominating them to do his bidding. Farrow social interactions involve bullying one's inferiors while seeking favor and avoiding the wrath of one's masters. Those who are mighty and clever prosper while the weak and foolish are fair game for abuse. In a never-ending cycle of challenges and retaliations, each farrow rises or falls in the loose hierarchy. It is not uncommon for a farrow to rise from beggar to chief and then be murdered as another aspires to replace him.

Farrow are most numerous in the otherwise unclaimed badlands of Cygnar and along the fringes of the Bloodstone Marches. Several mountain ranges and craggy hill regions shelter farrow villages, including the Dragonspine Peaks, certain sections of the Wyrmwall, and Caerly's Craig. The Thornwood has been home to farrow villages over the decades, although the present climate makes life difficult there. Migrations have pushed them north out of the warmer and drier regions into unpopulated areas of both Ord and Khador. They have settled as far north as the southern hills of Rhul, but the dwarven clans watching that border periodically drive them away. Even their most remote communities along the Bloodstone Marches have endured competition from the skorne Army of the Western Reaches.

Despite these threats, farrow are at greater daily risk from the predations of other farrow than outsiders. A farrow's worst enemies are neighbors envious of his belongings or status. Farrow become extremely possessive of claimed booty, whether it was won in battle, stolen, or pieced together from salvage. Murder between farrow over coveted items is common, particularly in a tribe with a weak chief who cannot enforce order.

For farrow tribes to survive, members must fulfill a number of required but undesirable roles, including menial labor. The most detestable work is delegated to those at the bottom of

ORIGINS OF THE FARROW

There has been some debate regarding the origins of the farrow. Their religion has no creation myth, though those of the Dhunian faith believe they emerged from her womb at some forgotten time. There is little mention of the race in human texts from the pre-Rebellion eras, leaving some to believe they arose by sorcery.

Most prominent theologians reject this idea on the grounds that the creation of an intelligent species is a power reserved to the gods. One likely theory is that the farrow were a natural species that migrated from uncharted territories and was subsequently modified and manipulated. They may have been bred specifically for battle, similarly to other enslaved creatures like the gorax.

Lending some credence to these theories has been the recent focused studies of the brilliant, if disreputable, Dr. Arkadius. Via a variety of surgical and alchemical techniques, he has modified them even further, including engendering abnormally large specimens. Through these efforts he has bred a variety of formidable warbeasts. Arkadius has discovered that not only are the farrow easily modified, but their flesh combines readily with that of other porcine species. Academia has yet to recognize the doctor's work, but the proof of his efforts is seen on any battlefield where his warbeasts are employed against his enemies.

their society, who comply out of fear. The most aggressive and skilled warriors and hunters seize positions at the top of the hierarchy, with a single warlike chief assuming ultimate dominance over the others. Any farrow capable of regularly acquiring food or other resources for the village gains respect, while those who must be supported by others are objects of scorn and shame.

Those who build and craft can also earn prestige, to a lesser degree, and may be able to barter these services for food or other goods. Of the farrow skilled at crafting, those who can build quality weapons are the most valued within a tribe. Farrow prefer to gather their food and rarely farm, having little patience for tending crops, although there have been exceptions where a tribe has learned to distill alcoholic spirits either for their own use or for barter. Many farrow tribes are semi-nomadic, following easy game and bountiful food reserves where and when possible.

Farrow warriors are not equally skilled, disciplined, or trained. In many cases those identifying themselves as warriors spend more of their time stealing and scavenging than fighting. In their language there is no distinction between the terms "warrior" and "brigand," as both are considered equally respectable occupations. Warriors are equipped to defend what they have claimed and naturally rise to positions of leadership over the less fit. Farrow take a pragmatic approach to both food and salvage; just as they will use or devour every last part of hunted game, they will strip down and seize anything left on a battlefield.

Arrangements are often made between farrow warriors and craftsmen, with warriors bringing scavenged materials to those capable of fabricating weapons. Farrow have proven adept at reproducing approximations of the weapons and tools of other races: farrow gunsmiths can hand-forge solid and reliable pig iron rifles from even cheap scavenged metal and have learned how to repair or rebuild other assets like cannons and steam engines.

MARKING TERRITORY

Farrow villages utilize impermanent structures of wood, clay, mud-covered straw, and scavenged sheets of metal hammered together in ramshackle fashion. When these structures are destroyed by enemies or natural disaster, the farrow simply rebuild them. Despite this, the honor of a farrow chief is reliant on his strength to defend his territorial borders. Keeping intruders away is, in fact, the first and foremost duty of a chief, as few things enrage farrow more than violations of their territory.

When confronted by an encroaching foe a tribal chief must make the difficult decision whether to flee or dig in and fight. Farrow determined to protect their lands prove surpassingly tenacious. Warriors armed with improvised or raided weapons will hunker amid entrenched positions and defend them to the death. Perimeters will be fortified with

sharpened spikes, deep pits, and a variety of natural snares and traps. Both trollkin kriels and isolated human outposts have discovered the farrow possess boar-like stubbornness. All adult farrow are combat-ready, with only the very young and pregnant females kept from the fray.

Faced with overwhelming odds, a chief may opt to retreat. One who gives the order to flee—even before a clearly superior force—will suffer the consequences, however, enduring shame and considerable loss of clout among his warriors. This is often sufficient to force an immediate change in leadership, even if the decision to flee was necessary for survival. When his leadership is threatened directly, a chief must defend it with his life. Those who falter are either killed outright or else driven from their tribe.

The strongest chiefs are the ones most likely to seek additional profit by bartering their fighting skills to outsiders for a portion of the spoils of battle. Often, these arrangements allow a tribe to experience riches well beyond what they could seize through localized plunder. They will accept a wide variety of payment for their services, preferring weapons but also welcoming food stores, raw materials, and access to better lands.

MYSTICAL TRADITIONS

Farrow do not generally enjoy long lives, but exceptions exist among a tribe's mystics, the most important of which are the shamans and the bone grinders. Farrow are rarely preoccupied with matters of faith except when reminded of their mortality. Most practice a variant of Dhunian worship, with short and simple rites. Funerals, births, and certain other occasions are occasions for shared prayer. They look to their shamans in times of battle to invoke blessings on the warriors. The most capable battle-shamans rise to positions of leadership and sometimes become chiefs.

Bone grinders embody a significant mystical tradition that incorporates the most pragmatic aspects of farrow life. Their ability to draw upon the innate power of slain beasts goes hand-in-hand with their belief that no part of an animal should go to waste. Even as meat is carved away to be eaten or smoked and stored, the grinders pull forth spiritual power left in the bones as a remnant of the once-living beast. Grinders can bolster the performance of warriors and chiefs with a loose approximation of alchemy that lets them create potent totems or unguents. Off the battlefield their mixtures can be used to speed healing after injury or relieve other bodily ailments.

Most chiefs also value these individuals for their advice and wisdom. Under a chief's protection, mystics are more likely to live longer than those farrow of other walks of life, and thus they can pass their practices down to the next generation. Some chiefs consider mystics meddlesome and cowardly, but where they are valued by the majority of a village's inhabitants it is necessary to afford them a modicum of respect.

THE THORNFALL ALLIANCE

For most of their existence the scattered and isolated farrow tribes existed in a state of perpetual infighting. This changed only with the rise of a giant among them, a farrow of such ambition, drive, and thirst for conquest he would change the very nature of his species. That farrow would become known as Lord Carver, the Bringer of Most Massive Destruction. Emerging from the dry hills northeast of the Black River near the Marchfells, Lord Carver immediately gained prominence by crushing every rival to appear before him, shaming chief after chief with displays of power. In his hand his cleaver became a blood-drenched symbol of might, and he was escorted by hulking porcine beasts he sent charging across the battlefield to annihilate his foes.

Lord Carver's inexorable rise to power did not happen overnight. After brutally subjugating several nearby tribes, he spent some time bartering his strength to nearby human military outposts and others who offered adequate pay. Lord Carver's contact with humanity, while profitable, left him forever disdainful of that species, which treated him with contemptible disrespect: Carver was viewed as any other farrow warlord despite his obvious supremacy. He determined he would unite his people in a war of conquest to prove his ultimate superiority.

Wherever Lord Carver marched, the farrow fell into line and obeyed him, but as soon as he moved on they descended into chaos. No one dared defy him openly, yet he lacked the organization and structure to maintain the momentum of his efforts. In battle he found himself hindered by the limited capabilities of his lazy subordinates.

As much as Lord Carver hates to admit it, the arrival of Dr. Arkadius enabled his dreams of larger conquest to become a reality. Ordinarily Lord Carver might have immediately dismissed the eccentric arcanist, but Arkadius had planned for the meeting with a demonstration of his unique genius. Before Lord Carver could even demand Arkadius explain himself, the doctor revealed his war hogs: tremendous hybrids of boar flesh and steam-powered weaponry picked from the battlefields of western Immoren.

LEADING THORNFALL WARLOCKS

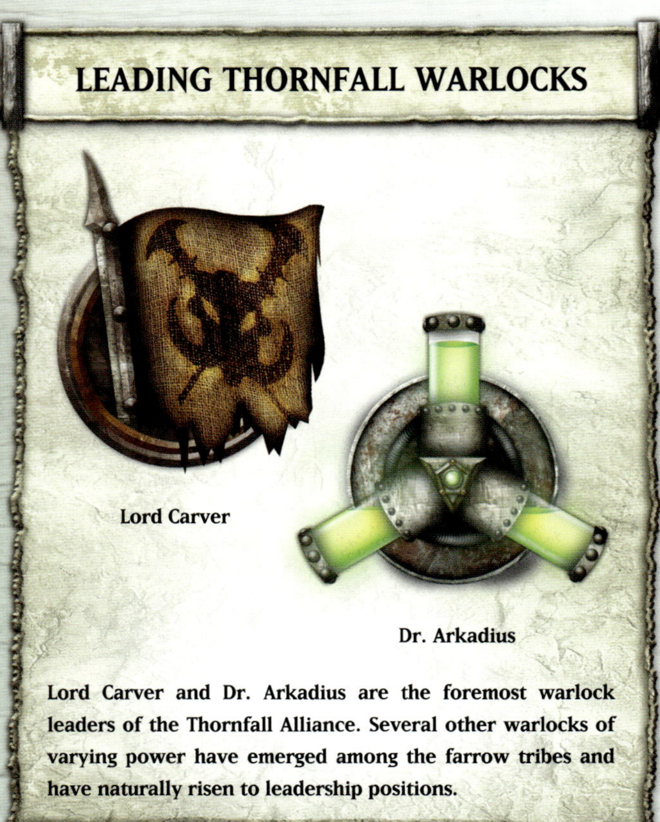

Lord Carver

Dr. Arkadius

Lord Carver and Dr. Arkadius are the foremost warlock leaders of the Thornfall Alliance. Several other warlocks of varying power have emerged among the farrow tribes and have naturally risen to leadership positions.

Lord Carver stands at the fore of his horde, but he is supported by countless tribal chiefs, each of whom considers himself the ruler of a petty fiefdom. These various chiefs defer to Dr. Arkadius, who has special stature among the Alliance even though many farrow are discomfited by his peculiar mannerisms, speech, and inexplicable arcane science. Even the greatest war chiefs are terrified of Arkadius, for they know his cunning is far beyond theirs. He has demonstrated the ability to shape farrow flesh as he wishes, and many who enter his laboratories emerge as something entirely other than what they once were—if they emerge at all. The chiefs obey Lord Carver to preserve their lives, but obedience to Arkadius is rooted in more insidious fears.

There is an ever-shifting order among the chiefs, as those deemed most valued by Carver command the respect of the rest and can pass down orders. Yet by and large the alliance's gathered warriors fight effectively in battle, each group looking to its own interests. Lord Carver is continually seeking ways to bring greater organization and tactical expertise to his army, including the recent adoption of banners to identify coherent tribal groups. He has also experimented with utilizing signals like whistles and flags to coordinate actions, although this has met with limited success.

Lord Carver immediately discerned the possibilities with such weapons at his disposal, and soon the doctor was ensconced within the warlord's inner circle as chief advisor. Relations between these two leaders is tense, but they formed the core of a new farrow alliance, possessed of both the raw sinew and the cunning to unite the tribes.

Lord Carver's army summoned the scattered chieftains to meet with him in the Thornwood Forest, at the site of an old battleground called Thornfall. The beleaguered farrow of the Thornwood had suffered considerably at the hands of Tharn, Cryx, Cygnar, and Khador, all of which had been battling across their territories. Lord Carver marched among them and seized control, intimidating the lesser chiefs into submission. Those few who resisted him were set upon by their own ambitious subordinates, each of whom subsequently bent knee to Lord Carver. This became the Thornfall Alliance, which Lord Carver intends to use in order to eventually stand as an equal against the human kingdoms—and then to conquer and subjugate them.

The great warlord has many feast halls where he assembles the farrow after victories and considers every village of his people his home. Yet his largest and greatest hall still lies in the hills of the Bloodstone Marches, just outside the region claimed by the Skorne Empire. Lord Carver does not rest long here but travels often to ensure the loyalty of those bound by pact into his alliance and to replace the fallen with fresh warriors from scattered villages.

LORD CARVER'S
FIRST ASSAULT BRIGADE COMPANY

LEADERSHIP
Lord Carver, BMMD, Esquire III
Chieftains Toklon, Makof, Klobin, Strod, Kortef, and Pargot

ASSETS
360 Farrow warriors
Dozens of Bone grinders
10-12 Razorback weapon crews
8 War hogs
12 Gun boars

Lord Carver continually watches the farrow in battle to find any who are particularly courageous, skilled, intelligent, and fierce even when cornered. Those who have impressed him may be selected for his personal fighting force, a group that battles alongside him at the front of every conflict. The name of this group has changed several times and likely will again as Lord Carver discovers military terms that appeal to him. At present they are the First Assault Brigade Company, a name that means little to those who carry its banner aside from pride of place fighting alongside their invincible warlord.

A few farrow remain in the First from Lord Carver's original rise to power, and they are veterans of dozens of bloody clashes among the tribes that resisted his vision of unity. At one point while fighting amid the hills of the Bloodstone Marches Lord Carver's force came upon a large skorne slaver army with a freshly captured haul of farrow. Those enslaved had once been enemies of Carver's old village, but the warlord descended upon the skorne and shattered their strength. He slaughtered the skorne to the last and freed the farrow, who immediately converted to his cause. They have become among the most ardent of his supporters, and several still serve in leadership positions among the First.

This fighting force prefers aggressive tactics and always initiates an engagement by leveraging maximum firepower against the enemy. Lord Carver unleashes his gun boars and razorback crews liberally at the outset to jar the enemy as much as possible before closing. Orchestrated volleys of pig iron fire follow, then he charges personally into the line alongside his war hogs. Farrow brigands are expected to lay on fire and switch to clubs when ammunition runs out or when the smoke of the onslaught makes picking distant targets impossible. Bone grinders provide their support but are also expected to wade into the fray with their heavy cleavers rather than lingering too far back. Lord Carver has made bloody examples of any he deems guilty of cowardice.

Casualties in this force tend to be high, as Lord Carver prefers to be in the thickest of the fighting personally. Still, the warriors and surviving families of those who fall within the First Assault Brigade Company are always well taken care of. This, added to the prestige of fighting alongside the warlord and earning the first pick of spoils, has made for a continuous stream of hopefuls seeking to gain Carver's attention.

DR. ARKADIUS
MINION WARLOCK

The gods may have created life, but nothing has been created which I cannot improve.

—Dr. Arkadius

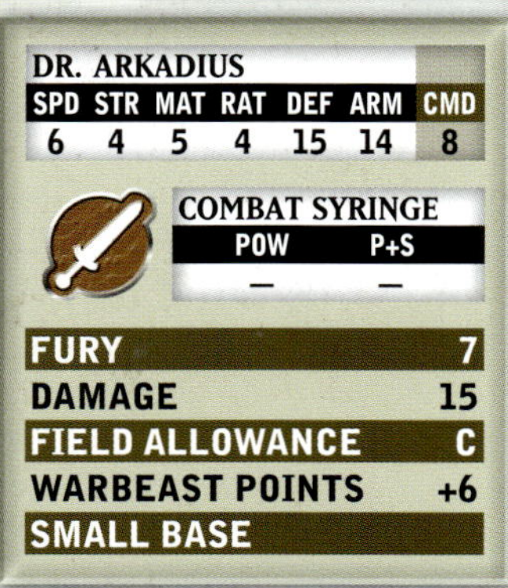

DR. ARKADIUS						
SPD	STR	MAT	RAT	DEF	ARM	CMD
6	4	5	4	15	14	8

COMBAT SYRINGE		
	POW	P+S
	—	—

FURY	7
DAMAGE	15
FIELD ALLOWANCE	C
WARBEAST POINTS	+6
SMALL BASE	

FEAT: MONSTER MAYHEM

Arkadius has delved into the minds of his freakish beasts with methods both cruel and cunning, and his mastery of their bodies and spirits is absolute. By his will and the power of his magic he can unleash the full destructive potential that might otherwise remain contained within mere flesh and bone.

Warbeasts in Arkadius' battlegroup can immediately frenzy. A model can frenzy even if it has already activated this turn and does not affect whether it can activate later this turn.

Minion – This model will work for Circle, Legion, and Skorne.

DR. ARKADIUS

Farrow Warlock – This model can have only Minion Farrow warbeasts in its battlegroup.

Maltreatment – Once per turn during its activation this model can remove 1 fury point from a warbeast in its battlegroup that is in its control area and add 1 fury point to its own current total. The warbeast suffers d3 damage points.

COMBAT SYRINGE

Magical Weapon

Ammo Type – Each time this weapon is used to make an attack, choose one of the following abilities:

- **Anesthesia –** A living model damaged by an attack with this weapon becomes stationary for one round.

- **Brain Damage –** A model damaged by an attack with this weapon cannot cast spells, upkeep spells, or use an animus for one round.

- **Mind Control Serum –** If a living enemy non-warcaster, non-warlock model is damaged by an attack with this weapon, immediately after the attack is resolved take control of the model. You can immediately make a full advance with it followed by a normal melee attack, then Mind Control Serum expires. The enemy model cannot be targeted by free strikes during this movement.

Needle – Do not make damage rolls to resolve attacks made with this weapon. A living model hit by this weapon automatically suffers 1 damage point. This weapon cannot damage non-living models.

The mysteries of life have eluded scholars for centuries, despite the best attempts of inept scientists. Their crude experiments invariably resulted in stunted, twisted things or, more often, utter failure. None of these academicians possessed the genius of Dr. Arkadius. A master of alchemy and the arcane, he possesses a rare brilliance beyond the ken of his less-gifted colleagues, who shunned him in their ignorance and prompted him to leave civilization behind.

SPELLS	COST	RNG	AOE	POW	UP	OFF
AGGRAVATOR	3	SELF	CTRL	–	YES	NO

While in this model's control area, friendly warbeasts gain Hyper Aggressive. (When a model with Hyper Aggressive suffers damage from an enemy attack anytime except while it is advancing, after the attack is resolved it can immediately make a full advance directly toward the attacking model.)

CRIPPLING GRASP	3	8	–	–	YES	YES

Target model/unit suffers –2 SPD, STR, DEF, and ARM and cannot run or make special attacks.

FORCED EVOLUTION	2	6	–	–	YES	NO

Target friendly living Faction warbeast gains +2 STR and DEF.

PRIMAL SHOCK	2	CTRL	–	*	NO	YES

Choose a friendly Faction warbeast in this model's control area. Target an enemy model within 8″ of the chosen warbeast and make a magic attack against it. The chosen warbeast is the attack's point of origin. If the enemy model is hit, it suffers a damage roll with a POW equal to the warbeast's base STR.

PSYCHO SURGERY	2	SELF	CTRL	–	NO	NO

Each model in this model's battlegroup currently in its control area immediately heals d3+1 damage points. This spell can only be cast once per turn.

TACTICAL TIPS

MONSTER MAYHEM – You can decide to have some warbeasts frenzy and not others.

MALTREATMENT – This model can exceed its FURY in fury points as a result of Maltreatment.

CRIPPLING GRASP – Because Crippling Grasp affects SPD, affected models cannot charge. Power attacks are special attacks.

At his remote laboratory, Dr. Arkadius has been able to indulge his surgical and scientific theories. He has found an ideal species for his great work, the primitive pig-men called farrow. Unconfirmed rumors suggest the species may have arisen from some earlier mystical manipulations of wild boars, an allegation supported by the ease with which farrow flesh responds to surgical intervention. He delights in how readily this species serves as an expression of his scientific artistry.

With the proper application of certain alchemical and electrical impulses, Arkadius encouraged farrow muscles to gain bulk, bones to lengthen and harden. Their bodies easily accepted organ and bone grafts from other porcine species. He has found their minds to be just as malleable. He can see great potential in the farrow but knows it will require time to unlock. He dreams of shaping the species into something sublime, leaving a lasting legacy on their minds and culture as much as on their bodies.

Arkadius watches the farrow with an artisan's eye even in battle, walking among them and taking every opportunity to spur on their huge beasts. He carries an array of alchemical serums he uses to improve the performance of his creations.

The doctor is ever mindful of chances to gather new specimens and materials, anticipating the day when those who once mocked his science will be at the mercy of the species he has molded into perfection.

Once their armies have been crushed underfoot I will carve a kingdom from the lands of men!

—Lord Carver

CARVER						
SPD	STR	MAT	RAT	DEF	ARM	CMD
6	8	7	6	15	17	9

SAWED-OFF SCATTERGUN			
RNG	ROF	AOE	POW
SP 6	2	—	12

HAND OF GOD	
POW	P+S
7	15

FURY	6
DAMAGE	16
FIELD ALLOWANCE	C
WARBEAST POINTS	+6
SMALL BASE	

FEAT: HOG HEAVEN

Lord Carver's ambition is boundless and his rage beyond comprehension. With a bellow he can instill in his followers a share of his devastating power. Their natural appetite for destruction and gluttony for violence stirs them to untold savagery.

While in Carver's control area, friendly Farrow models gain Overtake and an additional die on melee damage rolls. Hog Heaven lasts for one turn. (When a model with Overtake destroys one or more enemy warrior models with a normal melee attack, after the attack is resolved the model with Overtake can immediately advance up to 1″.)

Minion – This model will work for Circle, Legion, Skorne, and Trollbloods.

CARVER

(✴) **Tough**

Elite Cadre [Farrow Brigands] – Friendly Farrow Brigand models gain Combined Ranged Attack (⊘).

Farrow Warlock – This model can have only Minion Farrow warbeasts in its battlegroup.

Inspiration [Farrow] – Friendly Farrow models/units in this model's command range never flee and immediately rally.

SAWED-OFF SCATTERGUN

Both Barrels (★Attack) – This model gains +4 to the damage roll for this attack. This model cannot make additional ranged attacks with this weapon during an activation it makes a Both Barrels attack.

HAND OF GOD

(⊘) **Magical Weapon**

(⟫) **Reach**

SPELLS	COST	RNG	AOE	POW	UP	OFF
BATTEN DOWN THE HATCHES	3	SELF	CTRL	–	NO	NO

While in this model's control area, models in its battlegroup cannot be knocked down and gain +3 ARM but suffer –2 DEF. Batten Down the Hatches lasts for one round.

MOBILITY	2	SELF	CTRL	–	NO	NO

Models in this model's battlegroup currently in its control area gain +2 SPD and Pathfinder (⬦) for one turn.

QUAGMIRE	2	6	–	–	YES	NO

While B2B with target friendly Faction model/unit, enemy models suffer –2 DEF and cannot advance except to change facing.

RIFT	3	8	4	13	NO	YES

The AOE is rough terrain and remains in play for one round.

Never before in history has a farrow gained such a reputation as that of Lord Carver, the self-styled Bringer of Most Massive Destruction. Ruling over the growing herds of the farrow, Lord Carver is a grim figure. His lips curl in a snarl, openly displaying his disdain for other species. Bitterly jealous of the nations of man, the farrow lord savors cutting humans down on the field of battle. Someday he will wrest from the world the awe and adoration that is his due, and he will punish those who are too slow to kneel to him.

Lord Carver's brutal drive for conquest is born from time spent watching mankind from the fringes, seeing their cities and accomplishments with growing hate and envy. From the first time he sought to offer his services for coin, Lord Carver felt the supercilious disregard of humanity, how they viewed him as a lesser creature. He set out to subjugate his people in order to demonstrate to humanity that they must respect and fear him as a great leader. His conquest of the farrow allowed him a taste of what it will be like when he has brought the other, more hated, species under his hoof.

His vicious campaign culminated in the lesser warlords submitting to his will as generals in the would-be king's army. To demonstrate his worth, both among his people and to the humans seeking to hire his army, he borrowed honorifics in the human style and takes great pride in hearing his titles used to herald his return from battle. Gaining domination over his people was only the first step in a larger plan, for Carver will not be content until humans also bow to him.

To this day, Carver sometimes wishes he had killed the arrogant human who came to him and spoke of improving the farrow, both physically and culturally. Dr. Arkadius immediately seized upon Carver's expressed desire to forge his people into a weapon. While Lord Carver did not entirely understand all Arkadius' goals, the scientist proved himself by creating stronger beasts to assist in the escalating battles. The boastful human's counsel has proven valuable to Lord Carver, even as the farrow warlord mistrusts both his advisor's motives and his obvious intelligence. Lord Carver feels help from this human tarnishes his achievements, yet he cannot turn away the living weapons bringing him each victory. The farrow have made startling advances as a people on the strength of the doctor's schemes. One day Lord Carver will enjoy stringing Arkadius up and watching him bleed him out—but only once the obnoxious human has outlived his usefulness.

Lord Carver leads by example, exhorting his soldiers to rise above their origins and become greater. He rails upon any he deems lazy or lacking in proper enthusiasm for their

cause. He dreams of farrow fortresses and roads, of cities where they are the dominant race and humans are pushed to the dusty and windswept wastelands. When Carver is done, all western Immoren will either bow to him or be trodden under the hooves of their rightful master.

GUN BOAR						
SPD	STR	MAT	RAT	DEF	ARM	CMD
5	8	5	5	12	17	6

BIG GUN			
RNG	ROF	AOE	POW
10	1	3	13

OPEN FIST	
POW	P+S
3	11

OPEN FIST	
POW	P+S
3	11

FURY	3
THRESHOLD	7
FIELD ALLOWANCE	U
POINT COST	5
MEDIUM BASE	

GUN BOAR

Bacon – When this model is destroyed, each living warbeast B2B with it heals d3 damage points.

OPEN FISTS

Open Fist

For generations some unstable farrow bloodlines have occasionally yielded massive specimens of the race, which often lack the higher mental faculties of even the dullest typical farrow. Instead they display a fearsome temperament, an incredibly high pain threshold, and utter fearlessness. Farrow warlords have long made use of these creatures; even the smallest of the oversized throwbacks have battlefield applications. Physically powerful and possessing a rough intelligence just sufficient for basic weapons training, the gun boars are a significant asset to their people.

Once satisfied it is both a competent gun operator and easily able to distinguish friend from foe, the boar is fitted with a harness to carry the enormous cannon on its back. Despite the low-quality metals employed in sweltering open-air forges to craft them, thanks to their ingenious design these cannons are remarkably durable and able to resist the unpredictable combustion of the low-grade explosive propellants the farrow have seized in their raids.

ANIMUS	COST	RNG	AOE	POW	UP	OFF
COUNTERBLAST	2	SELF	–	–	NO	NO

When an enemy model advances and ends its movement in this model's command range, this model can make one normal melee or ranged attack targeting that model, then Counterblast expires. Counterblast lasts for one round.

On the battlefield, the gun boars support the advance of the farrow and war hogs, much like mobile artillery in a traditional fighting force. With a tug of its gun's lanyard, each gun boar fires an enormous shell stuffed with crude powder mixtures to punch yet another hole in the enemy's lines. These shells detonate on impact, showering the area with vicious shrapnel that grotesquely maims those it does not kill outright. Should an enemy somehow close with the gun boar, he finds no helpless artillery platform but instead a brutish hog eager to carve its next meal.

WAR HOG
MINION FARROW HEAVY WARBEAST

This project was but the first step in a greater journey, but the results are pleasing. I await tales of Lord Carver's victories gained at the cleaving blades of my war hogs!
—Dr. Arkadius

ANIMUS	COST	RNG	AOE	POW	UP	OFF
MASSACRE	2	6	–	–	NO	NO

Target friendly model can charge without being forced. When the affected model destroys an enemy model with a charge attack, after the attack is resolved it can advance up to 1″ and make an additional melee attack. Massacre lasts for one turn.

The enormous and deadly war hogs are among the most lethal of Dr. Arkadius' creations. Each beast is a fearsome expression of the doctor's genius. Carefully primed with alchemical reagents and then subjected to surgical experimentation, the beasts are powerful and violent creatures. Arkadius innovated unusual surgical techniques that enable him to keep his subjects alive while integrating powerful steam engines and other mechanikal augmentations directly into their flesh. This process has at times required hasty surgeries and the substitution of organs and limbs from other porcine subjects.

WAR HOG

Aggression Dial – This model can be forced during its activation to gain +2 STR for one turn but suffers d3 damage points.

GORE

Critical Knockdown – On a critical hit, the model hit is knocked down.

Though each war hog is a unique combination of flesh and machinery, all share a common purpose: the utter destruction of all who would oppose the Thornfall Alliance. War hogs can be pushed well beyond the limits of their flesh, their veins flooded with an alchemically induced rage that exacts a heavy toll upon their bodies.

WAR HOG

SPD	STR	MAT	RAT	DEF	ARM	CMD
4	11	6	1	12	18	6

WAR CLEAVER		
L	POW	P+S
	5	16

WAR CLEAVER		
R	POW	P+S
	5	16

GORE		
H	POW	P+S
	4	15

FURY	4
THRESHOLD	8
FIELD ALLOWANCE	U
POINT COST	8
LARGE BASE	

Even without a temporary overdrive of battle lust, war hogs are brutal in the extreme. Their bodies ripple with muscles further enhanced by clockwork and steam-powered pistons, a brilliant melding of beast and machine that makes them exceedingly formidable. To arm their war hogs, the farrow seek out the largest axes and blades carried by the warjacks of the armies of men. When set loose upon the enemy, a war hog's frenzy grows as its blood lust is inflamed with each kill. The massacre it unleashes is gruesomely punctuated by its grunts of delight and the screams of its victims.

FARROW BONE GRINDERS
MINION UNIT

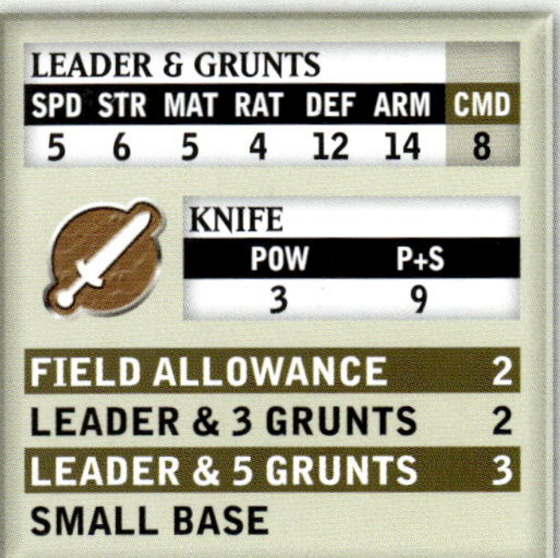

They leap right on a critter as soon as it dies, knives flashing, and cram bloody bones into sacks. Hope I'm a bit more discreet when I'm collecting my trophies.

—Alten Ashley

LEADER & GRUNTS						
SPD	STR	MAT	RAT	DEF	ARM	CMD
5	6	5	4	12	14	8

KNIFE		
	POW	P+S
	3	9

FIELD ALLOWANCE	2
LEADER & 3 GRUNTS	2
LEADER & 5 GRUNTS	3
SMALL BASE	

Minions – These models will work for Circle, Legion, Skorne, and Trollbloods.

LEADER

Confluence – This model gains a cumulative +1 on magic attack rolls for each other model in this unit that is within 1″ of it.

Magic Ability [6]

- **Arcane Bolt (★Attack)** – Arcane Bolt is a RNG 12, POW 11 magic attack.

- **Bone Magic (★Action or Attack)** – This model casts the animus of one friendly destroyed warbeast as a spell without spending fury points. This model cannot cast an animus with a RNG of SELF. This model must make a special attack to cast an offensive spell. Other spells are cast by making a special action.

- **Craft Talisman (★Action)** – Target a friendly warlock within 3″ of a model in this unit that is in formation. If the warlock is in range, when he casts a spell and is its point of origin, the spell gains +2 RNG. Spells with RNG SELF, SP, or CTRL are not affected. Craft Talisman lasts for one turn.

TACTICAL TIPS

MAGIC ABILITY – Performing a Magic Ability special action or special attack counts as casting a spell.

The lore of this type of shamanism has become a part of farrow culture and tradition. Certain particularly shrewd members of the species have used this skill to demonstrate their worth either to chosen allies or to the cruel masters who have subjugated them. The farrow have proven remarkably adaptable and considerably more intelligent than anyone might have anticipated. They have begun to thrive on the opportunities that have arisen in the battles erupting in the fringes of the wilderness and appear quite willing and even eager to fight alongside other species.

Necromancers and mortitheurges have proven the power inherent in flesh and bone lingers even after death. Bone grinders, well versed in skinning and deboning a wide variety of creatures, gather the parts of slain beasts in order to tap into the energies latent in the grisly trophies. Their methodology, part alchemy and part occultism, fuses mysticism and practical knowledge to craft a variety of charms and powders. Fresher corpses better suit the needs of bone grinders, who descend on the recently fallen with knives, cleavers, and serrated saws. Many mistake their industry as common butchery, but these craftsmen carefully select cuts of flesh, extracted organs, and marrow-filled bones for the mystical power within.

Bone grinders can carve lasting talismans of bone or grind them into powders and add such potent ingredients as blood, bile, and lymph to create a paste possessing tremendous mystical potency.

Once they've dug in, rootin' 'em out ain't easy. Give 'em some slop and good ground and they're here to stay.
—Alten Ashley

TACTICAL TIPS

Hog Wild – Yes, affected models can make ranged attacks, advance, and then use Dig In.

The farrow are stern half-man, half-pig creatures found throughout the wilds of eastern Cygnar, southern Llael, and the fringes of the Marches. Civilized communities loathe them and often spread unkind rumors of their piggish habits and inscrutable origins. This animosity has been exacerbated by the fact that farrow often prey upon and scavenge from remote villages, lumber camps, and traveling merchants. The people of the Midlunds despise them as freakish menaces to farmers and trade caravans alike.

In the recesses of the wilderness other groups are eager to employ these fierce and hardy soldiers. Noted for their thick hides and boar-like tenacity, farrow are as difficult to bring down as the wild animals they resemble. When armed with pillaged rifles, they are the equal of many frontline soldiers.

Minions – These models will work for Circle, Legion, Skorne, and Trollbloods.

LEADER & GRUNTS

Dig In (★Action) – This model gains cover, does not suffer blast damage, and does not block LOS. The model remains dug in until it moves, is placed, or is engaged. The model cannot dig into solid rock or man-made constructions. This model can begin the game dug in.

Prayers – The Leader of this unit can recite one of the following prayers each turn anytime during its unit's activation. Each model in this unit gains the benefits listed.

- **Heroic Call** – Affected models gain Fearless ⊛ and Tough ⊛ for one round.

- **Hog Wild** – Affected models can make one ranged attack this activation before this unit makes its normal movement. After their normal movement, models in this unit that make combat actions can only make melee attacks this activation.

- **March** – Affected models gain Pathfinder ◔ for one turn.

LEADER & GRUNTS						
SPD	STR	MAT	RAT	DEF	ARM	CMD
5	6	6	5	12	14	8

PIG IRON			
RNG	ROF	AOE	POW
10	1	—	12

CLUB	
POW	P+S
4	10

FIELD ALLOWANCE	2
LEADER & 5 GRUNTS	5
LEADER & 9 GRUNTS	8
SMALL BASE	

Several large farrow tribes came down from the Dragonspine Peaks to profit from the chaos in northern Cygnar during the recent Second Thornwood War. When both Fisherbrook and Stonebridge Castle were beset by Protectorate zealots, the military left a number of weapon caches exposed for plunder. The farrow were only too willing to seize these weapons and put them to good use.

Farrow maintain ties with both trollkin kriels and druids of the Circle Orboros. Farrow religion strongly resembles the Dhunian faith, and their shamans find much common ground. These races often barter for farrow services with needed resources such as blasting powder, food, or protection.

As with other species embroiled in these battles, the farrow have attracted the attention of Everblight's legion as well as that of the invading skorne. Both groups have been known to enslave the sturdy farrow for use as cannon fodder.

FARROW RAZORBACK CREW
MINION WEAPON CREW UNIT

LEADER						
SPD	STR	MAT	RAT	DEF	ARM	CMD
4	6	6	4	12	14	8

RAZORBACK			
RNG	ROF	AOE	POW
14	1	3	15

CLUB	
POW	P+S
4	10

GRUNT						
SPD	STR	MAT	RAT	DEF	ARM	CMD
4	6	6	4	12	14	8

PIG IRON			
RNG	ROF	AOE	POW
10	1	—	12

CLUB	
POW	P+S
4	10

FIELD ALLOWANCE	2
LEADER & GRUNT	3
LEADER: LARGE BASE	
GRUNT: SMALL BASE	

Minion – This model will work for Circle, Legion, Skorne, and Trollbloods.

LEADER & GRUNT

Dig In (★Action) – This model gains cover, does not suffer blast damage, and does not block LOS. The model remains dug in until it moves, is placed, or is engaged. The model cannot dig into solid rock or man-made constructions. This model can begin the game dug in.

RAZORBACK

Light Artillery – This weapon cannot be used to make attacks or special actions during activations this model moves. This model cannot gain the aiming bonus when attacking with this weapon and cannot charge. If this model attacks with this weapon during its activation, it cannot attack with any other weapons that activation.

Range Finder – While B2B with one or more grunts in this unit, this model gains +2 to attack rolls with this weapon.

A simple mechanism with no moving parts, the weapon is perfect for farrow. The launcher is little more than an extended metal tube employed to aim the unpredictable rocket flights. Each rocket requires an abundance of powder for propulsion and explosion; the farrow have recently raided enough from military convoys to fabricate many of the projectiles. Those farrow who prove calm under fire are trained in pairs to operate the razorback. Its volatile rockets must be handled with care, and razorback crews guard their equipment and ammunition from their fellow warriors.

The recent introduction of the razorback has shocked the enemies of the farrow, who were used to the species employing only crude fighting implements. Despite the relatively short range of their rockets, these crews are more than capable of blasting apart caravans and the walls of remote wilderness fortifications. The razorback crews are always important elements of these victorious supply raids, but their leaders grimace when they realize the powder expended in the attack might exceed anything gained by looting.

The camps of the farrow bristle with the forges and equipment to fabricate powerful, if crude, weaponry. While farrow are not known for their inventiveness, they excel at salvaging weapons from others, and several have demonstrated skill at breaking down enemy munitions and replicating them with stolen and improvised materials. The razorback was derived after seizing a variety of similar ordnance employed by other militaries, in particular Khadoran rockets fabricated in Llael. Trained teams of dexterous farrow work to assemble both the razorback launcher and its self-propelled rockets.

RORSH & BRINE

MERCENARY MINION FARROW CHARACTER SOLO & MERCENARY MINION FARROW CHARACTER HEAVY WARBEAST

It's best to ambush your troubles before they find you.
—Rorsh, translated from the farrow

SPELLS	COST	RNG	AOE	POW	UP	OFF
PIGPEN	2	SELF	*	-	YES	NO

While within 3" of this model, enemy models treat open terrain as rough terrain.

TACTICAL TIPS

LESSER WARLOCK – This model's type is solo, not warlock.

Rorsh and his gargantuan companion Brine wander the battlefields of western Immoren seeking sport and the opportunity for profit. The pair swagger into the most desolate war encampments on the fringes of the Iron Kingdoms to offer their services at a reasonable price—with no questions asked. A farrow of action, Rorsh is a cool professional unfazed by the horrors of war. He will calmly pause in battle, heedless of nearby dangers, to use his favorite tool of distraction: a stick of dynamite lit from his foul-smelling cigar.

Though Rorsh claims to be a mercenary, most civilized nations have branded him an outlaw. Only desperate communities on the fringes of civilization are willing to pay his bill. As merchants and lawmen from places as different as the frozen wastes of Khador and the blazing sands of the Protectorate can attest, Rorsh

Mercenaries – These models will work for Cygnar, Khador, Protectorate, and Cryx.

Minion – This model will work for Circle, Legion, Skorne, and Trollbloods.

RORSH

✠ Fearless

✠ Tough

Dig In (★Action) – This model gains cover, does not suffer blast damage, and does not block LOS. The model remains dug in until it moves, is placed, or is engaged. The model cannot dig into solid rock or man-made constructions. This model can begin the game dug in.

Diversionary Tactic (★Action) – Center a 4" AOE on Rorsh. Models in the AOE other than Rorsh and Brine suffer a POW 6 blast damage roll. After these damage rolls are resolved, Rorsh can make a full advance. If Brine was also in the AOE, it can make a full advance as well. They cannot be targeted by free strikes during this movement.

Farrow Warlock – This model can have only Minion Farrow warbeasts in its battlegroup.

Lesser Warlock – This model is not a warlock but has the following warlock special rules: Battlegroup Commander, Control Area, Damage Transference, Forcing, Fury Manipulation, Healing, and Spellcaster.

Souie! – If Brine is outside this model's control area during your Control Phase, before your models leach fury Brine can make a full advance directly toward this model.

RORSH						
SPD	STR	MAT	RAT	DEF	ARM	CMD
6	7	7	5	13	16	8

DYNOMITE			
RNG	ROF	AOE	POW
6	1	4	12

LEVER ACTION PIG IRON			
RNG	ROF	AOE	POW
10	2	—	12

CLEAVER	
POW	P+S
4	11

FURY	3
DAMAGE	8
FIELD ALLOWANCE	C
RORSH & BRINE	9
SMALL BASE	

and Brine are guilty of every form of opportunistic brigandage known to man and farrow alike.

Rorsh generally responds to his impressive list of crimes with a shrug and a grunt, as if to imply he has acted only as survival required. He has participated in several train heists in northern Cygnar, the plundering of military blasting powder stores, and the robbery of several small-town banks. Were he inclined to speak about such things Rorsh would admit to mixed luck in these exploits. Though he has always managed to evade capture, fate has conspired to keep a truly profitable score from landing in his lap.

Rorsh also prefers not to advertise the rather large number of victims he has left in his wake. He adopts the guise of a cheerful farrow with a knack for landing in trouble, but his deeds belie such innocence. It is no accident the enormous boar following Rorsh into battle has developed a taste for human flesh. Rorsh appears to be of the mindset that once a body is gone, a farrow can't rightly be guilty of murder. His preference for staying in lawless communities on the fringes of civilization has thus far supported his rationalization.

Rorsh keeps a tight lip. He understands several languages well enough but rarely speaks human tongues beyond what is absolutely necessary. Even words in the guttural farrow tongue rarely pass his lips; instead, he prefers to communicate by posture, glares, and raw intimidation. He conveys his meaning by a single chop of his hand, a feral grin, or a simple nod when offered a payment that meets his standards.

The independent farrow prefers areas that are dry, dusty, and windswept. He makes his way between small settlements along the edge of the Bloodstone Marches, Ternon Crag, the Dragon's Tongue, and the Hawksmire River. Throughout this region he has become known as a morally flexible freelance mercenary who is willing to work for nearly anyone so long as they do not try to impose their laws or regulations upon him. Occasionally younger farrow try to follow after him, hoping to learn from his example, but he does not abide hangers-on. Those who poke their noses into his business too persistently generally wind up disappearing. Despite this independent streak, Rorsh has found it profitable to offer his services to Lord Carver and his Thornfall Alliance. He refuses to stay too long and will not give up other lucrative contracts from any sense of farrow solidarity, but he pitches in alongside Carver's war bands with regularity. The warlord has demonstrated

ANIMUS	COST	RNG	AOE	POW	UP	OFF
PIG FARM	2	SELF	–	–	NO	NO

This model gains an additional die on melee damage rolls against living models. When this model boxes a living model with a melee attack, this model can heal d3 damage points. If this model heals, the boxed model is removed from play. Pig Farm lasts for one round.

TACTICAL TIPS

PIG FARM – Because the boxed model is removed from play before being destroyed, it does not generate a soul or corpse token.

a particular fondness for Rorsh, seeing in his silence a ready ear for his plans and ambitions. He mistakes Rorsh's silent disinterest for polite attention.

The boar Brine appears to be either a freakishly large farrow of unwholesome disposition or some sort of larger and less-intelligent porcine offshoot of the farrow species. Never far from Rorsh, the creature amplifies the threat represented by the formidable farrow. The boar's presence has made Rorsh a singularly compelling hire for those willing to meet his demands. The farrow might be deadly with a gun, handy with explosives, and wickedly efficient with his cleaver, but it is Brine that allows the duo to stand comfortably against larger threats like warjacks and warpwolves. The oversized pig has also been largely responsible for Rorsh's ability to evade the law. Even determined guardsmen, mercenaries, and soldiers cannot hope to stand against the huge creature.

Brine has the temperament of a wild boar, proving almost impossible to kill and becoming even deadlier when provoked by injury. Those who have fought the beast attest he can endure punishment that would kill any lesser creature. The more grievous his injuries, the more fearsome his relentless attacks become. His maddened squeals while lashing out with his tusks are terrifying, and his weight and bulk can shatter anything in his path.

The two have been an inseparable pair for as long as anyone can remember, and some insist they are utterly reliant on one another for survival. Feeding the creature without the benefit of the bodies left after battle would certainly be a chore. It is entirely possible that keeping Brine supplied with fresh meat is why Rorsh so diligently seeks work for hire and indulges in the occasional crime spree.

BRINE

Bacon – When this model is destroyed, each living warbeast B2B with it heals d3 damage points.

Companion [Rorsh] – This model is included in any army that includes Rorsh. If Rorsh is destroyed or removed from play, remove this model from play. This model is part of Rorsh's battlegroup.

Pain Response – While damaged this model can charge or make power attacks without being forced.

Pigheaded – If this model is destroyed by an enemy attack or if Rorsh is destroyed or removed from play by an enemy attack, before this model is removed from the table it can advance up to 3" and make one melee attack. When making this attack it ignores the effects of lost aspects. It cannot be targeted by free strikes during this movement.

Warbeast Bond [Rorsh] – Brine is bonded to Rorsh. During its activation, this model can charge or make a slam power attack against an enemy model that was damaged by a melee or ranged attack made by Rorsh this turn without being forced.

CLAW
Open Fist

GORE
Critical Knockdown – On a critical hit, the model hit is knocked down.

PAINTING MINIONS

Painting Minions is great fun and offers a nice break from the more regimented paint schemes of the faction armies. Many of these models use very bright and unique color schemes, which present painters with a wider range of opportunities for experimentation and exploration. These articles will provide a jumping off point for painting your own Minion models, but what we describe here is only the beginning. Of all the HORDES models, Minions offer the most avenues for allowing your creativity free reign.

Most Minions are modeled after animals, so looking at animal photographs is a great way to get inspiration for your color schemes. Another idea is to play with a particular faction's themes and colors; for example, you could paint skorne gatormen with manacles and whip wounds or make a blighted version of your favorite solo. Have fun with it; Minions are your opportunity to let your imagination run wild and to create models that will spice up your armies and your painting experience alike.

PAINTING TERMINOLOGY

BASECOAT

The initial coat of paint on which everything else will be built. It is important that the basecoat is very clean and every color is where it should be. Your shades and highlights will coordinate with the basecoat and main color choices.

DRYBRUSHING

The quick way to highlight a textured surface. Use a lighter color, but remove most of the paint from your brush by stroking the bristles on a paper towel until the paint is almost gone. Then carefully and quickly move the brush back and forth across the surface of the miniature.

GLAZE

A mixture of water and a small amount of ink that is applied in successive layers to subtly tint an area.

HIGHLIGHTING

A lighter color applied to the basecoat in the raised areas of a miniature to create the look of light hitting the surface. When highlighting in multiple steps, keep a little bit of the underlying color showing, overlapping them like the shingles on a roof.

SHADING

A darker color applied to the basecoat in the recessed areas of a miniature to create shadows. Exaggerating the shade and highlight colors will add to the visual appeal of a model.

WASH

A tinted mix liberally applied to the basecoat to create detailed shading. The wash will run into the smallest crevasses on a model and dry as a shadow, so it needs to be a darker color than the basecoat. The wash mix works well as **4** parts mixing medium, **1** part paint/ink, and **3** parts water.

BOG TROGS

Step 1) Basecoat the skin with a mixture of one part Thrall Flesh and two parts Moldy Ochre. Basecoast the scales with Battledress Green.

Step 2) Apply a wash to the skin using Battledress Green with mixing medium added for translucency. Wash the scales with Thornwood Green mixed with a small dot of Thamar Black.

Step 3) Return to the skin with the basecoat mixture and highlight some of the raised areas that were stained by the wash, leaving the recesses in shadow. Do the same with the scales, using Thornwood Green to highlight each scale and leaving a well-defined line of separation in the recesses.

Step 4) Mix Menoth White Highlight into the basecoat mixture and use this for additional highlights on the raised areas of the skin. Add Menoth White Highlight to Thornwood Green for the second layer of highlights on the scales and crest.

Step 5) For the final highlights, add more Menoth White Highlight to both mixtures and apply highlights sparingly to the highest points.

Step 6) Thin down a mixture of Skorne Red and Bloodstone to make a glaze and apply this in layers to the stomach and antennae. Use Menoth White Highlight to define the webbing of the spine crest.

- Thrall Flesh
- Moldy Ochre
- Battledress Green
- Thornwood Green
- Thamar Black
- Menoth White Highlight
- Skorne Red
- Bloodstone

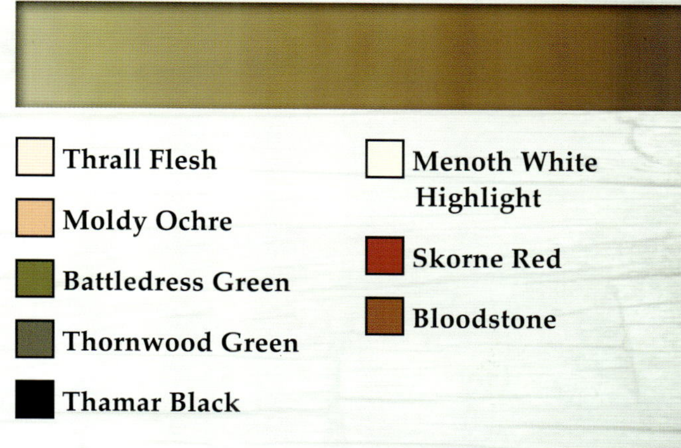

FERALGEIST

Step 1) Basecoat using a 50/50 mix of Wurm Green and Sulphuric Yellow. Apply four to five layers to avoid blotchiness.

Step 2) Add Sulphuric Yellow, some mixing medium, and water to the base color until it reaches wash consistency. Apply this wash to the whole model so that the details become apparent.

Step 3) Begin shading with Sulphuric Yellow in the recessed areas of the model.

Step 4) Add further shading with Menoth White Highlight mixed with Sulphuric Yellow and mixing medium.

Step 5) With the depths of the feralgeist glowing brightly, highlight the raised surfaces of the model with Wurm Green.

Step 6) Mix Ordic Olive with some Wurm Green and a drop of mixing medium. Use this to apply darker highlights to the raised areas of the model.

Step 7) Heavily dilute Yellow Ink with water (1:15). Apply this glaze to the entire body in multiple layers, being careful to avoid any excessive pooling in the crevices.

Step 8) To bring out the contrast, apply a final shade of Menoth White Highlight, making sure to avoid dominating the previous layers. Highlight the most pronounced raised areas with Ordic Olive. Use these highlights sparingly to define and separate areas of the model, such as the hair, fingers, and ribs.

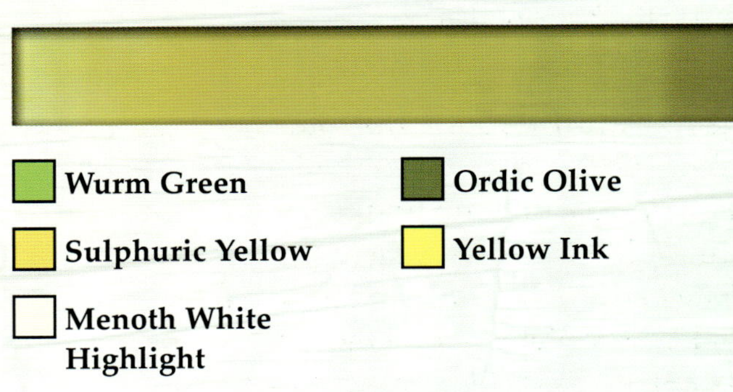

- Wurm Green
- Sulphuric Yellow
- Menoth White Highlight
- Ordic Olive
- Yellow Ink

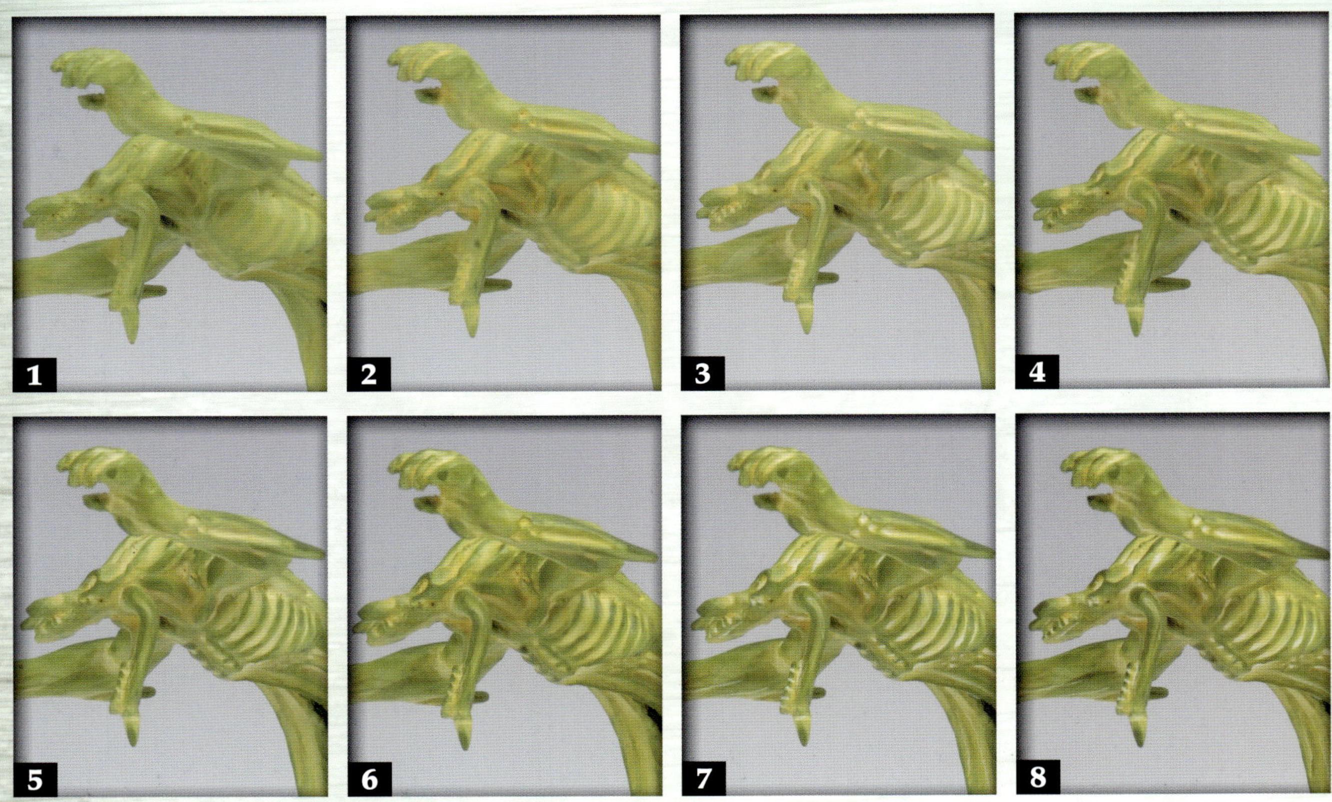

TATZYLWURM BODY

Step 1) Basecoat the inner skin of the wurm with a mix of equal parts Arcane Blue and Frostbite plus a touch of Wurm Green. Basecoat the underbelly plates with a mix of Frostbite and Meredius Blue. Paint the back plates with a mix of Meredius Blue and Gnarls Green.

Step 2) Take the color you used for the basecoat of the inner skin, mix in some Menoth White Highlight, and use that mixture to highlight the inner skin. Shade the underbelly plates with a mix of Meredius Blue, Blue Ink, and Turquoise Ink. Shade the back plates with Coal Black mixed with a touch of Thamar Black.

Step 3) Add Turquoise Ink, Blue Ink, and Green Ink to the color you used to highlight the inner skin and use that mixture to shade the inner skin. Add Morrow White to the underbelly plate base color and use that to highlight the underbelly plates. Add Underbelly Blue to the back plate base color and use that to highlight the back plates.

- Arcane Blue
- Frostbite
- Wurm Green
- Meredius Blue
- Gnarls Green
- Menoth White Highlight
- Blue Ink
- Turquoise Ink
- Coal Black
- Thamar Black
- Green Ink
- Morrow White
- Underbelly Blue

1

2

3

MIXING INKS WITH PAINTS

One way to achieve vibrant colors is to add a bit of ink to your paints. That's the trick with the Tatzylwurm. The ink mixed into the shades and highlights is what gives it such a rich color. Ink goes a long way, so be mindful and add only a little at a time until you have what you want. Want a stronger red? Simply thin your red with a spot of Red Ink. Want your yellow to pop? Mix in some Yellow Ink. Experiment with inks, and you will be surprised at the colors you can produce.

GATORMEN POSSE

Step 1) Basecoat the underbelly with a mix of Ryn Flesh and Hammerfall Khaki, plus a dot of Moldy Ochre. Basecoat the rest of the scales with a mix of two parts Cryx Bane Base, two parts Wurm Green, and one part Cryx Bane Highlight.

Step 2) Lay down a wash to define all the small scales in one quick step. For this use equal parts Ordic Olive and Armor Wash with a drop of water and a drop of mixing medium. Apply this evenly over the entire surface of the skin with as little pooling as possible.

Step 3) Shade with a mix of Thornwood Green, Armor Wash, and Battlefield Brown on the undersides of the model, using a second brush to blend as you go. You can also use a fine tip brush to paint this mix carefully into the cracks between scales for extra definition.

Step 4) Use a mix of Hammerfall Khaki and Menoth White Base to highlight the individual scales on the belly. Apply a line highlight along the top of the scales in shadow, and simply fill in the rest of the underbelly scales. Use a mix of Wurm Green and Thrall Flesh for similar highlights on the rest of the scales. To give the illusion of light glinting off of wet scales, apply small dots of Menoth White Highlight to the scales on the highest parts of the model. Position the dots in the upper corner of each scale and keep them as small as possible.

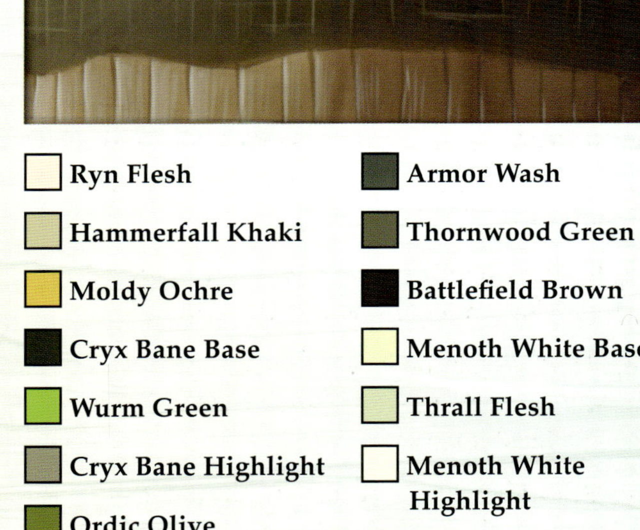

- Ryn Flesh
- Hammerfall Khaki
- Moldy Ochre
- Cryx Bane Base
- Wurm Green
- Cryx Bane Highlight
- Ordic Olive
- Armor Wash
- Thornwood Green
- Battlefield Brown
- Menoth White Base
- Thrall Flesh
- Menoth White Highlight

FARROW FLESH

Step 1) Basecoat the flesh with a solid layer of Gun Corps Brown.

Step2) Shade the recesses of the flesh and hair with a mix of Greatcoat Grey, Cryx Bane Base, and Gun Corps Brown.

Step 3) Use a mix of Gun Corps Brown and Rucksack Tan to highlight the flesh and fur.

Step 4) Mix Thamar Black and Umbral Umber and blend this toward the tips of the hair. Blend Khardic Flesh into the snout and lips.

Step 5) Highlight the snout and lips with Midlund Flesh. Basecoat the teeth and nails with Menoth White Base.

Step 6) Shade the teeth with Ember Orange. Apply Bloodstone to the deep shadows and recesses of the teeth. Highlight the teeth with Menoth White Highlight.

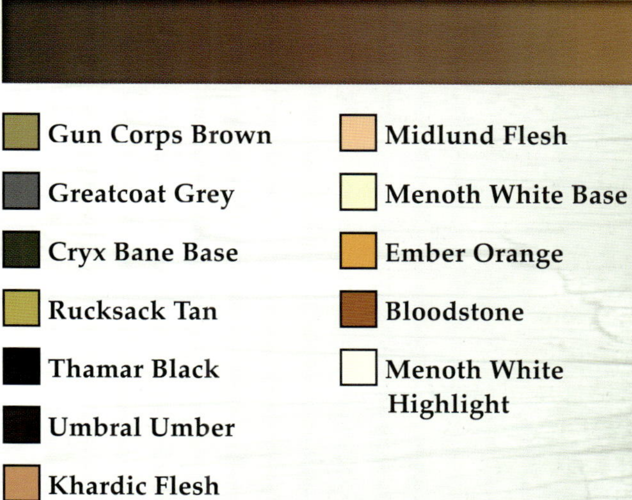

- Gun Corps Brown
- Greatcoat Grey
- Cryx Bane Base
- Rucksack Tan
- Thamar Black
- Umbral Umber
- Khardic Flesh
- Midlund Flesh
- Menoth White Base
- Ember Orange
- Bloodstone
- Menoth White Highlight

1

2

3

4

5

6

CALABAN, THE GRAVE WALKER
Warlock

BLOODY BARNABAS
Warlock

LORD CARVER, BMMD, ESQ. III
Warlock

DR. ARKADIUS
Warlock

SWAMP GOBBER BELLOWS CREW
Unit

TOTEM HUNTER
Solo

ALTEN ASHLEY
Solo

VIKTOR PENDRAKE
Solo

SAXON ORRIK
Solo

RORSH & BRINE
Solo & Heavy Warbeast

GUN BOAR
Light Warbeast

WAR HOG
Heavy Warbeast

FARROW BONE GRINDERS
Unit

FARROW BRIGANDS
Unit

GATORMAN POSSE
Unit

CROAK HUNTER
Solo

IRONBACK SPITTER
Heavy Warbeast

WRONG EYE & SNAPJAW
Solo & Heavy Warbeast

BOG TROG AMBUSHERS
Unit

BLACKHIDE WRASTLER
Heavy Warbeast

BULL SNAPPER
Light Warbeast

GUDRUN THE WANDERER
Solo

BRUN CRAGBACK & LUG
Solo & Heavy Warbeast

DAHLIA HALLYR & SKARATH
Solo & Heavy Warbeast

LANYSSA RYSSYL, NYSS SORCERESS
Solo

FERALGEIST
Solo

THRULLG
Solo